TIME RUNS OUT

TIME RUNS OUT

EDDIE R PORTER

authorHOUSE®

AuthorHouse™
1663 Liberty Drive
Bloomington, IN 47403
www.authorhouse.com
Phone: 1-800-839-8640

First published by AuthorHouse   07/09/2011

ISBN: 978-1-4634-2894-5 (sc)
ISBN: 978-1-4634-2893-8 (dj)
ISBN: 978-1-4634-2892-1 (ebk)

Library of Congress Control Number: 2011910957

Printed in the United States of America

Acknowledgments

Writing the tale of the little town of Glencoe, Oklahoma, was a fun experience, and the more I wrote, the more memories kept coming back to me. Glencoe is typical of other small communities in Oklahoma or any other state. The people are hardworking, mostly blue-collar, and believe in family, God, and country; and like a lot of places, the teenagers are creative when it comes to "entertainment." The community is close-knit, and the people all know each other and in a sense become part of your family.

The citizens know what Hillary Clinton wrote is true: "It takes a village to raise a child." Glencoe was my village, and I will always be grateful for the opportunities I had while living there and for having my "extended family." It is because of them as well as my own family that today as a grown man I am who I am, for better or for worse.

I also want to acknowledge that material relating to the history of Glencoe was provided by D. Earl Newsome in his book, titled *The Story of Exciting Payne County*.

Me in 1966

CHAPTER I

The Town

D RIVING DUE EAST SEVEN miles out of Stillwater, Oklahoma, you come to the junction of Highways 108 and 51. Stillwater is the home to Oklahoma State University and is known for having sold more Budweiser beer in a one-block span than any other block in the United States, except for one block in New York City. The university is also known for its dominance in NCAA wrestling, having won numerous national championships, the flags are hoisted high in Gallagher-Iba basketball arena for all to see. Next to these trophies are two NCAA men's basketball championship flags for titles won in 1945 and 1946. Legendary basketball coach Henry Iba led the United States Olympic team to victory in an earlier year. Just down the street from the arena is "the strip," located on Washington Street near campus and where a few years earlier the first "streaker" in the country ran bare-butt naked. The strip is a hangout for university students to drink beer, eat pizza, and party, and the main night for these party's

1

is always Thursday, because students leave the campus on Friday to return to their home communities.

As a driver gets to the junction, they either keep going on 51 and end up in Tulsa or turn left, exit on Highway 108, and enter the small town of Glencoe, six miles down the two-lane highway. The roadway was constructed in 1958 after a few of Glencoe's leading citizens traveled to the state capital in Oklahoma City to petition Governor Raymond Gary for a paved highway to be constructed between Glencoe and Highway 51 to increase trade and commerce between Stillwater and their town.

Glencoe, unlike other communities in Payne County, had its founding not related to the Oklahoma land run of 1889 or the Sac and Fox land opening of 1891. Glencoe owes its existence largely to the Santa Fe Railroad. In 1899, the Eastern Oklahoma Railway began laying a track from the territorial capital of Guthrie into modern-day Payne County. Before the railroad was completed in 1900, the track came from Ripley, across Boomer Creek, to Stillwater, and then on to Glencoe and Pawnee.

With the railroad came the organization of a town site company and the sale of town lots. Buildings sprang up almost immediately, and the little town of Glencoe took form. On December 6, 1899, a post office was officially established and a postmaster appointed. In the beginning, the town's name was spelled "Glenco," but it was changed when the newspaper started, the *Glencoe Mirror*, operated and owned by Hunter Williams. He demanded Glenco have an *e* attached to the end of the name, but the US Postal Service refused his demand—at least, until he announced that the town had been named after Glencoe, Scotland, a beautiful pass in Argylshire. The post office finally gave up, and on June 28, 1901, the name was officially declared to be "Glencoe."

In 1967, the town almost could have been declared a ghost town, except it did not meet the official qualifications for those who make such decisions. The town population was four hundred and twenty, the same as it had been the past thirty years. Over time there had been plenty of deaths but also plenty of births, keeping the population stagnant. The community has its mainstay families, whose relatives had founded the town. The Clarks, the Shells, and the McGinty, Driskel, Childers, Porter, and Honeyman families, to name a few, were thankful their pioneer relatives had had enough vision and wisdom to settle the community where there was good grazing and farming land and fertile soil, the town having been nestled between the Black Bear Creek to the north and Camp Creek to the south.

After the town was founded it quickly grew to include a fabric shop, hardware store, locker plant, filling station, tag agency, and two grocery stores. The town was also home to the Jack Bunn Mercantile Company. That business drew customers from miles around; some came to shop, others just to see the unique store. Bunn's store was said to carry everything from high-button shoes to the latest styles. Shelves from floor to ceiling lined the store from front to back. Glencoe was being hailed as the best town in Payne County, second only to Stillwater. Its goal was to become a trading center for surrounding communities of West Point, Lawson, Yale, Jennings, Crystal, and Ingalls.

As soon as Glencoe was settled, citizens began plans for a school. The founders temporarily set up a tent as a schoolhouse. Eighteen students representing nearly all grades attended. The next morning, the pupils discovered their school had blown away, along with their books and supplies.

Williams, owner of the *Glencoe Mirror*, jumped on his horse and rallied the men of the community. He decided the sure way to avoid the school's being blown away again was to build an underground classroom. Within two days they had dug a fourteen-by-eighteen-foot hole four feet deep. Above the ground they put three feet of logs around each side, making a room seven feet deep.

After a few years the *Glencoe Mirror* folded, but the slack was picked up by the *Pawnee Chief*, a weekly newspaper always delivered on Thursdays. The *Chief* depended on a volunteer from town to provide information about the town and its citizens. Zola Murphy, English and Journalism teacher, always gave the latest news to the paper on

Tuesdays. She announced who had visited whom—usually on a Sunday afternoon—where they went for the day, where they ate (often including the menu being described); along with other tidbits of news like who had had a cow escape from the pasture and how they had herded it back to the pen.

By 1967, the town had changed. Stores closed and new ones opened, and Glencoe no longer had as many stores as in its earlier days. But now the town had a modern bank, two filling stations, a high school, an elementary school located across the highway from the high school, and a fire department. The town also had one police officer, whose job was to set traffic traps in order to increase revenue for the town's treasury.

Fire Station   **Police Station**   **Main Street**

As drivers travel on Highway 108 from Stillwater via Highway 51 toward Glencoe, they come to a flat piece of road measuring a quarter of a mile long. Along this straightaway is the Gilcrease Junkyard. Tom Gilcrease lives across the road whenever he is not at "the 'yard," as it is known. The 'yard has hundreds of old cars piled on the eighty-acre lot. Customers who need a spare part go to the "car cemetery" to pick up what they need in the way of used components. When the 'yard is closed for the night, it is secured by a chain-link fence with a lock attached to keep out the unwanted. For those persistent to enter they are met by a large German Shepard who is not afraid to show his teeth and take a sample of meat from the intruders' leg or arm.

The straightaway is also used by local teenagers to test the speed of their car against all comers in the quarter-mile run. The cars line up on a marked piece of highway, wait for the flag to be thrown by an observer, then take off, hoping their car is up to the task and can take the abuse. Following each race, bets are settled, and often a new challenge is issued for another day.

Although no one has ever died while racing, a local man died one weekend night when he lost control at the top of the hill after flying through the quarter mile. Chester—which is not his real name—walked with a limp but nevertheless had a desire to become a movie star on the big screen in Hollywood. The popular television show *Gunsmoke*, starring Dennis Weaver was a hit and led the ratings for nighttime television at the time. After going west, Chester returned to Glencoe without a script or ever having a chance to make it in the movies or television.

The night of his death he had been partying at a local pub in Stillwater. Late that night as he steered his yellow Firebird convertible with its black soft-top rag toward Glencoe, after turning on Highway 108, he hit the gas to blow out any dust that may have settled in the exhaust. As Chester topped the hill doing 110 miles per hour, the car went airborne. landing in a bar ditch, he was killed instantly.

Estie Stokes, a local who lived at the top of the hill, heard the crash and reported it sounded like a sonic boom when the car hit. He called the EMS in Stillwater, the fire department, and the sheriff's office. "Too late," announced the deputy who was first on the scene.

The EMS pulled up with its siren and lights blaring. The paramedic got out, took one look at the car, and then radioed to the Stillwater hospital, "We will be bringing in a body, but we won't have our lights on, code for the patient is dead."

When Chester was taken to the emergency room, the emergency doctor announced he was DOA. Strode Funeral Home was notified; they were to have the body ready for the funeral, scheduled three days later.

The First Baptist Church of Glencoe hosted the funeral, the church Chester had attended on occasion but always on Easter and Christmas. The day of the funeral was a warm September day, and a majority of the townspeople attended. The pastor had to set up extra chairs for the overflowing crowd of people to sit. The preacher spoke about heaven and hell and assured Chester's loved ones he had entered the gates of heaven and was being cradled in the arms of Jesus at that very moment. At the end of the service, the pallbearers prepared to move the casket from the church to the small cemetery located south of town, but before they did, the attendees listened to the choir sing "Amazing Grace" followed by "Down by the River," two favorites of the Southern Baptist parishioners.

Chester had been the only person to leave Glencoe to try to make it big in Hollywood at least up until 1967.

The two men cruising along the highway were new to the area; no one had seen them before. The strangers did not know anyone in the town and were not known by the locals. Why they chose Glencoe was a mystery. As they entered the city limits on the south end of town, they slowed down to twenty-five miles per hour, the city speed limit set by the volunteer city council. As the strangers passed by Roy Gant's filling station they saw the billboard with the price of a gallon of gasoline being forty-five cents.

Lyndon Johnson was president of the United States, and the cost of goods was beginning to rise due to the war effort. Many Americans disagreed with Johnson's policy toward Vietnam, while others agreed with his plan to keep South Vietnam a free, democratic country. Besides, Johnson had told the country that if the Communist North Vietnamese took control of the South there would be a domino effect, and other countries in Southeast Asia would fall to the Communists. Johnson had declared, "Now is the time to stop the Commies."

In Glencoe, with a few exceptions, the townsfolk thought Johnson was right and were willing to sacrifice to help the president; loyalty to the government was not in question as the locals pondered the questions of morality, of right and wrong.

In the meantime the Southern states were engaged in the civil rights movement; blacks were demanding equal rights, the same rights as their white brothers and sisters. The black population was no longer willing to buy a bus ticket in the front of the bus and then disembark and go to the back of the bus to enter and find a seat in the "colored" section. Riots were occurring daily in places like Selma and Birmingham, Alabama; Philadelphia, Mississippi; and Baton Rouge, Louisiana.

Glencoe was an all-white community, and what was going on hundreds of miles away did not concern the local population. The bigger issue was how the Panthers would do in basketball during the season.

After the car with the strangers reached a sign pointing to Main Street, the only paved street in town, they turned left. To their left was the then-vacant home of Charles and Lizzie Shell. Lizzie had passed away the year before, and Charles eight years earlier, so their home was for sale. It would be a good purchase for a young couple, newly married or looking to get started with a family.

As the car continued west down Main Street it passed the First Baptist Church on the right and the United Methodist Church on the left. Minister Dale Stockton, the Methodist preacher, could turn a soul righteous before the congregation could blink an eye. Stockton was popular in town; he was young, good-looking, and a family man. The minister knew all his flock by name, each of their problems, and who needed guidance.

Although Glencoe was without many businesses, the little town had plenty of churches, including the Church of God and the Church of Christ. Glencoe's Methodist church had not always been free of scandal; the first had come in the summer of 1900 with the founding of the church. The reverend Granville Lowther had delivered the dedicatory sermon and was considered a likely prospect to become permanent minister. But then he was charged with heresy. Lowther had shocked church officials with his biblical interpretations. He contended that the creature in the Garden of Eden that persuaded Eve to partake of the forbidden fruit was not a serpent, but another man who had not yet "come into consciousness with God." At the Arkansas Church Conference Lowther was charged with "disseminating doctrines contrary to and subversive to the doctrines of the Methodist Episcopal Church." Lowther was suspended from the ministry, and Glencoe had to look elsewhere for a preacher.

Across from the street from the Baptist church sat the town's water tower, rising seventy-five feet in the air and overlooking the little town. The tower was rusty and in need of a good paint job, having last been painted twenty-five years earlier. Painted on the water container was the word *Panthers*, along with a depiction of the town's mascot, painted by John Clark just within the past few years. John had done such a good job with his artistry that the panther appeared ready to strike anyone who got near it. Painted over the rust were also the names of teenagers who had climbed the water tower and braved not getting caught.

Past the water tower sat the town fire station. The volunteer department had one old fire truck that was started one time a week to keep the battery charged. Going west past the fire department one found the business section of town. On the left was an old, rock building built just after the town was founded by Dr. C. H. Beach. The building was small and in the 1950s was used by a visiting doctor, who tended to minor aches and pains. By 1967, however, it was empty and was considered a historic site by the townspeople.

The town had two grocery stores, owned and operated by the two grocery men, Ed Shell and Orville Sawyer. Each man competed for the business of the locals, and although each store was small and neither had a wide variety of groceries to choose from, each had loyal customers who would never consider shopping anywhere else. Besides, each man would carry a customer's bill and never apply pressure for them to pay monthly or on time.

Directly across the street from the Shell grocery store was Kenneth Shell's soda fountain shop. Kenneth are Ed were brothers who had lived in Glencoe their entire lives, and although each was beginning to get up in age, neither had considered moving from Glencoe to where doctors and hospitals were abundant. The soda fountain was a popular hangout for the teenagers; teens met at the fountain daily after school, after sporting events, or just dropped by unannounced. The fountain had a long bar with bar stools where patrons could sit and drink a coke, order an ice cream soda, or enjoy a snack. Most teenagers, however, went to play pool, listen to the latest music on the jukebox, or sit at a booth with their boyfriend or girlfriend.

The local bank, Glencoe State Bank, was owned and operated by Clarence McGinty, who had been the bank president since 1941. Before that he was with Farmer's

National Bank in Ripley, another small town in Payne County. All the townspeople knew that Clarence had survived three bank robberies. The Glencoe State Bank was the last business to be remodeled and updated with beige brick; other businesses continued to have old, faded rock covering their building facades.

Next to the bank was the post office, run and managed by Aileen Shell, wife to Kenneth and sister-in-law to Ed. Aileen always made sure the mail was delivered daily and on time. Her rural mail carrier was Marion Clark. Marion had been with the post office for twenty years and knew everyone along his route. He knew not only their first names, but the names of their spouses, who their parents were, and how many children each customer had.

One of two gas stations sat on the north side of Main and was the last business before a driver had to decide to make a U-turn, steer left, or turn right; heading northward or southward put the driver on a dirt street. Tommy Focht owned the filling station and was married to Sue Hrabe.

Sue was a real beauty and was elected Founder's Day Queen in 1966. The holiday was celebrated each year in September to commemorate the founding of the town. To become queen required an electoral process: each girl competing wore a swimsuit, climbed up onto the back of a flatbed truck, turned around for all to see her figure, and then stepped back down the stairs, exiting the truck. The girl receiving the most whistles and applause was declared the winner. The queen wore the crown for one year, and then the election process began anew and another queen was selected. The election of the queen was a popular one and each of the young ladies in town always looked forward to competing for the coveted crown and title of Miss Founders Day.

On the south side of town was a gas station owned by Roy Gant and his wife, Gladys. Rumor had it that Gant was selling the station, and folks thought Leland and his wife, Brenda Ross, would buy the station. They were newly married and had been seen meeting with Gant at the local café. Since Gant always had the coldest pop in town, everyone was hoping Leland would keep the same soda cooler, the type where to get a pop you have to maneuver the pop bottle through an obstacle course before having it firmly in your grasp, ready to drink. A bottle cap opener was attached to the square box for convenience.

At the end of Main Street, going north on the dirt road, one would drive past a self-service car wash that more times than not did not have enough soap to thoroughly clean a dirty vehicle. For twenty-five cents you got a five-minute spray. If you kept going you would pass the home of Freddy and Joann Clark, a bright, white house set among the cooling trees planted around the home. The Clarks had one of the newest houses in town. Past the Clark homestead, making a few curves along the way, you'd come to the Lyle Cotton

Gin. Cotton had once been a major agricultural product in the area but had begun to give way to wheat as the choice for local and state farmers.

Watermelons were also grown nearby, by Andy Murphy, and plenty were available in the community as well as surrounding communities. Andy always had the finest watermelons in the county. His melon patch provided enough watermelons for the local teenagers to "borrow" a few on Halloween night, where inevitably a melon could be found on Main Street, busted wide open. Besides being a local watermelon grower, Andy was considered the local expert on forecasting the weather and knew when the last freeze of the year would be. Andy always said the land would be good for planting anytime after April 10.

As the two men came into town around sundown, they drove slowly past the bank. Driving slowly did not draw attention, as everyone drove at a turtle's pace down Main. The men reached the end of Main and made a U-turn to go back down the street, and as they got back to the bank, they pulled in between the yellow stripes and parked. They remained there in their car for ten minutes then slowly backed out and left town.

Each evening the local saloon was visited by ranchers, farmers, construction workers, and oil riggers. Each dropped in to visit to talk about their problems or share good fortunes, and afterward they wet their whistles, usually more than once, and then the cards and dominoes came out for a little friendly competition. On this evening no one had noticed the car parked in front of the bank.

CHAPTER 2

The Lecture

THE NEXT DAY GLENCOE appeared as it always had: a lazy little town, but a nice place to call home. The locals met at the café to swap stories, talk about Panther sports, and drink coffee. Always in attendance were Bill Childers, local propane dealer and little league baseball coach; Loyal Honeyman, state game ranger; Frank Driskel, milk truck driver for a distributor in Stillwater; Kenneth Shell; and Homer Howard, school superintendent. Mr. Howard was always referred to as *mister*, even by the adults, because of his education and the way he dressed: black suits, black shoes, black tie, and white shirt. The core group was often joined by others who were in town, usually doing their banking, or when business was slow.

On this day, Monday, school was to begin; the new school year always started the first Monday following Labor Day. The school lacked air conditioning, and starting in early September was thought to be a good choice. The temperature was not as high as in August, and the teachers and students could do their work without wiping the sweat off their brows, even though it was still typically pretty hot during the first two weeks of the new school year. But to start earlier would be unbearable, and to boot it would cut into the farming and ranching business, as sons helped their fathers with the crop harvest or planting. The compromise was for teachers to open the windows in their classrooms to allow the air to circulate.

Howard was a strict superintendent, a no-nonsense sort of administrator who lacked a sense of humor—at least, that was the way the students saw things. Mr. Howard had been superintendent for one year and was about to begin his second. He was responsible for 97 high school students and 112 elementary students and was proud of the fact that he knew every student on sight and knew who to keep an eye on, who might cause him a problem.

The principal, Mr. Wallace, had received his certification as an administrator the year he'd become principal of Glencoe. Wallace was young and still had an eye for the young female teachers. To add to his duties, he coached the boys and girls basketball teams and in the spring was the driver's education teacher.

Superintendent Howard had, the year before, threatened the high school students with expulsion if the school was damaged on Halloween night. He'd given his speech during an assembly on the day of Halloween. He told them not to be stupid and that if they did anything to vandalize the school; he would call the Payne County sheriff's office. Glencoe did not have a police department, except for one low-paid officer; the town could not afford it. In fact, the town could not afford but a few services other than water, which came from pumps scattered around town. For example, in the winter if a heavy snow swooped down on the little town, making the streets impassable, it was up to each resident to clear a path to their house; no street maintenance crew existed.

When he gave his speech, Mr. Howard had no evidence a plan had been hatched; he just felt it in his bones. The day after Halloween he was the first to arrive at the school, and above the entrance door in bold, black letters were the words "Sing Sing" spray painted on the dull, brown rock. Howard was furious; his blood pressure began to rise, and his face turned red. The students had called his bluff.

As the school buses lined up in front of the school to let the students off, Howard met each one of them at the front door. He was not smiling or greeting the students in cheer, he was giving each a hard stare. As the students passed without saying a word, they went directly to their first-hour classes, even though the school bell had yet to announce that class had begun. After the yellow buses with the words "Glencoe School District, 101" on their sides let their students off, they slowly moved toward the "bus barn," where they would stay until it was time to pick up the students from school and return them home.

Following the school bell's having rung, Howard announced on the intercom for all students to assemble in the school gym "Right now." Once the students began to assemble, he took the high ground, going directly to the stage located in the gymnasium. Now standing several feet above the students as they sat on the bleachers, he swatted at a fly that had been circling his head and had landed on his nose.

Before Howard began, he asked the principal, Mr. Wallace, to come to the stage and stand next to him. Wallace enjoyed the spotlight; he was cocky as he strode up on stage, brushing his hair from his forehead. As Howard began, it was immediately clear that no loud speaker would be needed; he made sure he was heard. The students knew the lecture would be serious. They had been warned.

"When I arrived at the school house this morning I found the school vandalized," stated Howard. "I had warned each and every one of you not to destroy school property and to behave like human beings and not animals, but I guess some of you just won't listen, so I want you to know that all of you will be treated as though you were responsible until the guilty are caught." When you start to complain and feel you are being mistreated by the restrictions I am going to impose maybe you will then point the finger to the guilty. It is because of them that I am doing what I am going to do."

Howard then told the students there would be no leaving school property at noon, "No one is allowed to leave and go downtown for lunch, you will either eat at the school cafeteria or not at all. You will not be allowed to congregate in the hall between classes and anyone late for class will be sent home with homework until I decide differently. Now, maybe you will remember when I say something you need to listen."

As Howard spoke, Wallace would nod his head in agreement, supportive of the boss and his plan to get to the bottom of the vandalism. Howard ended by telling the students he would be calling the sheriff as soon as he finished talking. He told them he would not tolerate pranks, that he considered the wrongdoers to be criminals, and he reminded the students they represent the school 24/7. He would not stand to be embarrassed by their actions.

Following twenty-two minutes of lecture, the students were dismissed to return to class. As the students left, none of them spoke a word; they walked quietly until they arrived at their classrooms.

Standing at the top of the stairs in the doorway to her English class, Zola Murphy was waiting for the students to arrive. Ms. Murphy was in her early sixties, wore black, horn-rimmed glasses, and on this day had her hair braided in a ponytail. Murphy was known to be a fast driver, and when seeing her approach on the roadway, drivers would scurry to get out of her way. She had been at the assembly when the superintendent had lectured the students, and seeing his reaction she knew he was a very angry man.

Ms. Murphy read the great poets and often would quote Edgar Allan Poe. As the students began to be seated, she blurted out, "The mind can make a heaven out of a hell, or a hell out of a heaven."

Linda Childers, one of four girls in the class and a straight-A student, asked Ms. Murphy what the quote meant. Murphy said, "On this day it means there is hell to pay."

After English the students had five minutes to gather their books, go to the restroom, get a drink, quickly meet up with a friend, and get to the next class. In the hall Mary Ann Shell met Sandy Honeyman, Marilyn Childers, Andrea Shelton, Janine Chaffin, Marietta Cavett, and Carlene Murphy to talk about their cheerleading practice, scheduled for 5:30 that evening.

At the same time, the junior and senior boys moved quickly to the gym for physical education and the beginning of basketball practice. In attendance were Bill Hodge, Eddie Porter, John Clark, Randy Robinson, Gary Mitchell, Dale Lyle, Randy Clark, Larry Shell, Larry Murphy, Mike Crawford, and Mike Wiseman. Upon seeing them, Mr. Wallace ordered the boys to the locker room to dress in gym shorts; he did not greet the students with a hello or give any signal he was glad they were there. When the boys returned fully dressed for activity, Wallace told them to run ten laps around the gym, followed by twenty-five sit-ups, fifteen push-ups, and then another five laps around the court. The gruesome workout had begun.

Muscles were aching and the boys were having trouble breathing, winded. Once they reached center court, they were leaning down with their hands on their knees, exhaustion setting in. After the physical torture was finished, Mr. Wallace demanded they sit on the bleachers. "I have something to say," he told the captive audience. "If any of you were part of the vandalism to the school last year, you can count on me finding out. And when I do, you will be finished with sports, do you hear me?"

None of the players looked at each other during his speech or when he finished; there was no movement. Wallace would not be given the satisfaction on this day.

Pawnee was a town of forty-five hundred residents and the county seat for Pawnee County. The town was centered around on a square, where engraved into bricks were the names of foreign war veterans from the county who had served. A World War I cannon sat in the courtyard, and a flagpole proudly displayed the American flag that was hoisted each weekday morning at 8:15 a.m. and taken down at 5:00 p.m., the time always remaining the same, since Mary Jo Price was in charge of the flag and she would only raise or lower it during her work hours, Monday through Friday. The flag did not fly on weekends. The town had never purchased a light to shine on Old Glory, which would have made it legal to fly the flag at night.

Just down the street from the courthouse was Clicks, a fine establishment which served only the finest steaks. People came from all around to eat a Click steak. The front door was always closed and locked. The door had a peephole so the owner could look through it when someone wanted to enter; only whites were allowed in the establishment.

At the south end of Pawnee was the National Guard Armory. The guard had grown in numbers since the war in Southeast Asia had started to heat up, as young men had joined up rather than be drafted into the Army.

Inside the armory was a large, concrete floor used as a skating rink on Friday and Saturday nights. Located just fourteen miles from Glencoe, Pawnee was a regular hangout for the teens. The rink was perfect for skating, the music was lively, and all the latest hits were played, as well as golden oldies from the past.

The teens of Glencoe found it a good place to go "hook up" with the opposite sex without it being obvious, no date required. No one ever went to the rink without having made sure a large contingent of other teens would be there. When it was time for a boy to pick a girl to skate with, the girls would line up against the wall, a boy would skate over and take her hand, and off they went. The same procedure was used when the time came for a girl to pick a boy. So as not to be embarrassed, it was always known who would pick who; besides, what could be more embarrassing than to pick a partner, offer your hand, and be turned down?

As the skaters began their dance, the lights dimmed and change from white to red, green, blue, and yellow. The rink was smooth and not dangerous, except for if some whiz kid skating faster than you cut in front, barely missing your skate, and down you went. If you were lucky you could prevent your partner from falling along with you. From time to time someone would fall, mostly from not paying enough attention to their skating, causing a roadblock. Others usually were skilled enough to make their way around the crash site and keep skating. It was embarrassing to the person who fell, however, and not a good way to impress the girl he was with.

A disc jockey was always at the rink playing music. Usually the DJ would ask for a request, make a few jokes, and then spin the 45. The top songs played were "Respect" by Aretha Franklin, "Light My Fire" by The Doors, "Purple Haze" by Jimi Hendrix, "Somebody to Love" by Jefferson Airplane, and "A Whiter Shade of Pale" by Procol Harum. Teenagers who were dating steady always asked for "Sunshine of Your Love" by Cream. The slower-paced songs were couples' favorites. Slow skating with an arm wrapped around the midsection of your date was one way to show others your like for that particular person. Another was to hold hands while skating.

The Glencoe high school published a weekly newspaper that was circulated to all the students. The paper featured Panther sports, announcements the school wanted the students to be aware of, and the student favorite, a section where a teenager could dedicate a song to his or her special friend. The only rule for making a dedication was to use initials, and the first paper issued for the new school year had EP dedicating "Teddy Bear" to DM.

At the skating rink no one ever requested soul music, such as "Soul Man" by Sam and Dave. The teens had little exposure to the black population and knew little of black culture or black history. It was not until it became known that Chuck Berry was black that requests were made for black rock and roll musicians and bands to be played. WKY Radio, 930 AM in Oklahoma City, played rock and roll and could easily be dialed in during the daylight hours. The teenagers always tuned into WKY when disc jockey Danny Williams was on the air. At night, KOMA, 1520 AM, had the strongest signal, and Ronnie Kaye was the listeners' choice. Ronnie Kaye also starred as host of a popular Saturday dance show in Oklahoma City, and all the teenagers turned on the television set to watch for the latest dances and crazes.

Chapter 3

The Three Evils

G LENCOE IN 1967 WAS an all-white town; there were no "coloreds" who lived in or near the town, even as the civil rights movement was making headway in the South. Big cities were on fire, local cops used fire hoses, to break up riots, and Governor George Wallace of Alabama stood in the doorway of the University of Alabama to prevent two black students from enrolling. In Mississippi the governor used the same tactic. Although both governors were unsuccessful, mostly because the federal government intervened, the sentiment of the South had not changed.

In Glencoe the only event in memory involving blacks happened in 1901. The townspeople apparently felt a need to do something about blacks. None had settled in the town, but a half dozen worked for the Santa Fe Railroad, which came through town regularly. The town took action that it thought would have a lasting impression on the black population.

When the morning train came puffing in on June 24, 1901, the engineer and crew were startled at what appeared to be a black man hanging from the railroad bridge. A closer look revealed that the figure was a life-size dummy, but the newspaper, the *Mirror*, said it had served its purpose. The *Mirror* reported, "The negro question about which there was so much concern last week seems deader than a hammer. This seemed to be sufficient warning to the colored men not to leave the right-of-way nor go pestering around town. The Santa Fe sent in five or six Negroes who have been working without molestation and will not be molested . . . as long as they keep their place and do not attempt to become citizens of the town."

The event had occurred sixty-six years earlier, and a new generation of citizens living in town had little interest in what was happening hundreds of miles away—a distant land, thought the locals who met every morning at the café.

KSPI Radio in Stillwater did not report on the latest current events; they focused on giving information to farmers and ranchers about the grain futures and cattle and hog prices, and they played music listened to by the older generation. From time to time they would have a local musician play a song or two on the radio; Max Porter played guitar and was a frequent guest.

To learn about national and world events, the townspeople of Glencoe had to turn their television sets to watch Chet Huntley and David Brinkley on NBC, or Walter Cronkite, anchor newsman for CBS. The latest national polls said Cronkite was the most trusted man in America. Every night Cronkite had a lot on his plate, reporting on the civil rights movement, the war in Vietnam, and the hippie movement, which started in San Francisco and had moved to the East Coast. Cronkite gave the viewer grim news nightly on the number of Americans who had been killed in Vietnam, and he was slowly beginning to insert his own views on the war, a problem that later confronted President Lyndon Johnson as the public began to oppose the war.

As the American government became more and more involved in Vietnam, Congress began to seriously talk about establishing a lottery draft. Just the talk about a draft led more young men to college to get an education deferment or to the local National Guard to enlist for a six-year stint.

Johnny Marlow, who lived north of Glencoe and who had graduated two years earlier from a neighboring town, voluntarily enlisted in the Army. John was sent off to boot camp and later was taught to fly helicopters. After his specialized training he was sent to Vietnam, where he was killed in action after having been in the country less than three weeks. It was reported that John had been flying a helicopter when he'd received word of GIs pinned down and needing help evacuating the wounded. As John circled the helicopter to head to the action, he was shot down, the copter's impact into the ground killing him instantly.

Johnny Marlow's father was working in the field on his farm, and he became ill at the exact time his son was killed. Mr. Marlow left his tractor and walked to the house to lie down. A few days later, word came about his son having been killed in action. John had not graduated from Glencoe but was known in the community as a well-behaved young man, intelligent, and loyal to his country and family. He was considered a hero by the people of the town. He was the first local victim of what became known as "Johnson's war."

The hippie movement had yet to invade Glencoe but was nearby in Stillwater on the campus of OSU. The hippies were said to have long hair and to be drug users; they dressed as though they needed money for clothing and looked as though they were in need of a good shower, they drove Volkswagen cars called "Beatles" and enjoyed "pot" more than work. The people of Glencoe were friendly and gave little attention to the "new generation". The men at the café talked about their growing up years and felt the hippie movement was just a fad, nothing to be concerned about as the teens in Glencoe respected their parents, adults in general and were "raised" the correct way.

In Glencoe the only teenagers with long hair were Bill Hodge, Keith Hodge, and Randy Clark. Each boy had good parents who always knew what they were up to. The boys were not considered hippies; they were on the basketball team and popular among the people in Glencoe. Bill Hodge, the team's center, often scored twenty points and had ten or more rebounds at the end of a game. He was all hustle.

When Glencoe won a game on the road, Bill was often harassed by the opposing team's fans, shouting things like, "If you come back here we will kick your butt!" Others could be heard saying, "Come back and you will never step on the court. Got that, kid!" But Bill was not the kind to be intimidated, and he continued to play hard and with enthusiasm.

The team was composed of both country kids and kids from the town. The country boys worked in the hayfields during the summer to earn spending money for date night or to buy the latest fashions in clothes. They would lift bales of hay weighing eighty pounds or more, toss the bales on the back of a truck, stack them, and then put the hay in the hot, dry, dusty hay barns. Each hay hauler earned five cents a bale—not a lot of money, but then the price of gasoline and other goods had yet to rise. The kids from town mostly made their money from moving lawns or doing odd jobs for the locals.

CHAPTER 4

The Investigation

A S THE SCHOOL YEAR began with enthusiasm, Howard was still distraught from the vandalism just the year before. He had yet to discover who the criminals were. He strongly believed they were still in school this year, and Halloween was just seven weeks away. He had kept his promise to call the sheriff's office to report the vandalism and to launch an investigation, but little had been discovered.

The deputy, Gregg Russell, drove his 1962 Ford to the school, parking in the front for all to see his presence. He stepped out, wearing black jeans, black shirt with a silver star, black boots, and a straw hat. The deputy was ready for cooler temperatures as he was proud to wear his Silver Belly Stetson hat, long black trench coat, and to top off his attire with a new revolver the sheriff had special ordered for him along with other deputies. Russell was intimidating to look at; his gun was visible for anyone to see, and he stood six-foot-two and must have weighed 245 pounds. In his jaw was a wad of tobacco, and his front teeth were stained yellow. Russell was not they type to play a joke on or to give him a hard time".

As Russell entered the school he went straight to Howard's office, closed the door to the hall, and told the secretary he was there to see the superintendent. After he entered Howard's private office, he took a seat. Howard, sitting behind his desk, extended his hand for a handshake. After the two settled in, the deputy told Howard he had been assigned to the case and had just begun his investigation.

When Howard asked if he had any news to share, the deputy said he was there to interview the seniors and juniors. "I will interview all of them," he said, "but I am mostly interested in the boys; they will be the ones to have done a criminal act. The girls might know something, though. Boys can't keep their mouths shut." He then told Howard, "I want to interview them first as a group, and then I will meet with them individually."

Howard smiled; the deputy had a plan, and at last he was getting some action. Howard had promised the students he would get to the bottom of the crime and that those responsible would pay dearly. Howard grinned and thought to himself, *They will pay.*

Russell asked Howard if he had a paper cup; he needed to spit the tobacco juice from his mouth. Howard got on the phone and dialed the extension for his secretary. "Bring me a paper cup," he instructed the secretary, adding eagerly, "and get on the intercom and have the juniors and seniors assemble in the gym Tell them to be there in ten minutes and to take a seat on the bleachers."

"Yes sir," said the secretary.

After a few moments the secretary brought in the cup to the deputy, then she left the room, closing the door behind her. Russell said, "I am sure someone knows something about the crime. I will be able to unravel this thing when I conduct my interviews. If the guilty party doesn't confess, someone who knows will spill their guts."

As the students filed into the gym and took their seats on the bleachers, they saw the deputy and Howard enter. The students instantly knew the deputy was there because of the prank a year ago. *Howard will not let up*, they thought, murmuring to each other.

Howard began by introducing the deputy as one of the finest investigators in the law enforcement business and knew how to solve a crime. Howard then told the students they would be interviewed and that they should cooperate. "If you don't, I will consider you responsible for the vandalism," he warned. Then he turned it over to the deputy.

As Russell began he introduced himself by name and chose to be confrontative and intimidating believing he could look into the eyes of the guilty and quickly determine who was responsible. The deputy said he had twenty years of experience investigating crimes and that he considered the vandalism to be a felony act, then he quoted the state law defining vandalism. He told the students those responsible were considered by the law to be criminals, "But I say not only are they criminals, they are also thugs and hoodlums." He then instructed the students to remain seated. "I will interview each of you individually, and when I am finished with one, I will come for another to question." He asked if they understood. The students listened intently to Russell and knew he was not a man to play around with. As they continued to sit and wait for their name to be called he stood looking at each one of the junior and seniors, staring them in the eyes without saying a word.

No one said a word, but there were plenty of nods indicating that the students not only understood but knew what would happen if they failed to follow the deputy's instructions. The deputy then asked the superintendent which office he could use for the interrogations. Howard told him, "You can use my private office. It is quiet, and you will have ample privacy."

The deputy asked for Dale Lyle to accompany him. In the meantime, Howard instructed Principal Wallace to remain with the students. "Make sure they do not talk among themselves," he said. "If they do talk, I want you tell me immediately; they can talk to the deputy if they have something to say."

Howard then left to go downtown to the café. He wanted the locals to know what was happening; he had made a promise to get to the bottom of the crime, and by informing the café group, he knew word would get out that he was making good on that promise, even a year later.

As Howard entered the café the usual group of men was present. Frank Driskel looked up, saw Howard, and asked if school was out. "No," said Howard, "I just wanted you boys to know that I am about to get to the bottom of the vandalism. I have a deputy at school right now, a good investigator, he will find out who was responsible and then I will take the appropriate action." Bill Childers asked Howard if there were any new developments. "No," said Howard, "except I am more convinced than ever this thing will get settled once and for all."

Before the deputy began the interview he told Lyle if he knew who the guilty party was to speak up, it would be the only way to stop everyone from being interviewed. He then said, "If you had a part in the vandalism you should speak up now, and I will make sure you are not punished as severely as the others. Now let's begin. Did you have any part in the crime?"

"No," said Lyle.

"Do you know who did it?" asked the deputy.

"No," the boy said again.

"Would you tell me if you did know" ask Howard.

"I would tell you if I knew," said Lyle, "but I don't know and I don't have anything else to say."

The interview went on for fifteen minutes and Russell had not learned anything new. He then dismissed Lyle and asked for Eddie Porter.

Porter entered and was told to sit down. The same questions were asked, and each time Porter said he had nothing to do with the incident and did not know who had been involved. At one point Porter told the deputy he should spend more time on real crime, that whoever had done the spray painting had been playing a prank and the deputy should not consider it as vandalism. The deputy became furious and said, "If I don't get to the bottom of this I will have all of you hauled into the jail where you can sit without bail, wait for a hearing that will take at least thirty days, and when convicted spend the next two years in a reform school for boys in Helena! How would you like that?"

"Do you know what a reform school is asked Russell?"

"I know," said Porter, "but why would I go there if I didn't do it?" asked Porter.

"Because I think you do know and besides I don't have to prove beyond a shadow of a doubt that you did it, all I have to do is present enough evidence to make it look like you did" said Howard.

Porter apologized and was sent back to the bleachers. As the deputy continued interviewing, he became more and more upset. When he finished with the seniors, he asked for the juniors. However, now he changed his tactic and told the interviewees he had information about who committed the crime, a witness; he just needed the guilty to confess, he said. He told them Perry Tucker, the school janitor, had seen the act being committed.

Tucker lived across the street from the school, and all the students knew him, a quiet, gentle man who was always friendly to the students. The deputy told the interviewees that on the night of the crime Tucker had heard a noise, opened the curtains to his window, saw a ladder standing at the school entrance, and saw spray paint being applied to the rock. The deputy then said all he needed was for each person not involved but who knows the perps to speak up. "I am not here," said the deputy, "to find the guilty. I know who they are. I am here to get those who know about the crime, those who know who did it and have yet to spill the beans." As the students listened they became more and more nervous. Did the deputy know who did it, if he does why is he still here, why doesn't he take the guilty party away thought each of them as they continued to sit and wait?

As each student was sent back to the bleachers, they sat without saying a word; they were unable to tell those yet to be interviewed of the bombshell that was about to drop in their lap. Once the deputy completed all the interviews, he had not gotten a single confession, he had not learned anything new, and the students all stuck to their story of not knowing who had committed the crime.

Howard observed one of the interviews by sitting in after he'd returned from the café, as proud as a peacock at having told the members of the morning group what was happening. He knew he would be considered a local hero; maybe even get a pay raise when the guilty parties were found. As Howard listened to the deputy describe how a witness had seen the crime of the century, he became more and more pleased, although he was disappointed no one had confessed to knowing who had committed the crime.

After the interviews, as Russell debriefed Howard, the superintendent asked the deputy if it was true he knew who had committed the crime. The deputy winked, shook the man's hand, and said, "I will be back in touch."

After Russell left in his car with the markings, "Deputy Sheriff, Payne County," Howard asked to see Perry Tucker. Tucker was told what the deputy had said—that he, Tucker, knew who had done the crime. Tucker looked at Howard and told him he went to bed each night at 9:00 p.m. and slept like a rock; he had not seen or heard anything. The deputy had lied.

CHAPTER 5

The Bank Robbery

THREE DAYS INTO THE new school year, the Stillwater press had as its lead story, "Coyle Bank Robbed." The radio station KSPI reported the bank had been robbed in broad daylight by two gunmen. The men had escaped with a sizeable amount of money, and bank employees and customers had been terrified. The station then went back to reporting their usual news, the daily market price of cattle and hogs, and enjoyed two guitar instrumentals by Max Porter.

The newspapers reported no one had been seriously injured, but the bank president had been roughed up. The way the reporter told the story, upon entering the lobby of the bank, the lead robber approached one of two cashiers and slipped her a threatening note. The second robber took a position by the front door and appeared nervous, according to the eyewitnesses. The first robber whispered to the cashier, "Make any noise and people are going to die." He told her not to say a word, to act normal, and to not alert anyone of what was happening.

The cashier read the note and dropped the cup she had been holding, spilling coffee on the floor. The noise startled the customers and the second cashier, who was sitting at a nearby table. The bank president, whose office had a direct view to the teller windows, got up to see what had happened. As soon as the cup fell, the two robbers pulled their guns and began to tell everyone to get behind the counter. They didn't spot the bank president until he saw what was happening and made a beeline to his private bathroom.

One of the robbers went to the bathroom, where he found the door locked. "Come out by the count of three or I will kill everyone in here," he demanded.

The president opened the door and stepped out; the robber took his pistol and hit the president across the face with its butt. He led the president to the others and hogtied him and then the others. One cashier was first escorted to the front door, where she was handed a pre-made note to tape on the glass of the door. The robber then told her to close the blinds and go back where the others were being held. The note read, "Sorry for the inconvenience. We will be closed for the remainder of the day but will open again tomorrow at 9:00 a.m."

The robbers then made their way to the safe and found it unlocked. They took what cash was on hand, put it in money bags, and then stepped back to where the hostages were being held. "Say one word in the next hour and you will die, I will make sure of that," said the lead robber as he and his partner checked the ropes holding the hostages' legs and hands, making sure they were secure. The two then walked out the bank door, knowing they had less than an hour to make a getaway before the hostages would free themselves and alert the police.

Soon one hostage wriggled free from the rope, and she immediately began untying the others. Once all had been freed, the three customers left the bank through the front door, screaming, "Robbery, Robbery!" to anyone in earshot. The bank president picked up the phone and called the police department.

The town of Coyle had one officer and one chief. The chief was off for the day, taking a "mental health day." The deputy had been parked near the school watching for speeding motorists. He had just returned to the office when the call came in. "This is Officer Davis, Bryan Davis," said the policeman as he answered the phone. "How can I help you?"

"This is the bank," said the bank president. "The bank has been robbed!"

"What?" said Davis. "You mean someone stole something?"

"That's right, we were held hostage by two gunmen, get over here quick."

"I'll get on it," said Davis while his hand began to shake and he began to perspire.

Within three minutes the officer had peeled out on the street in front of the station, heading toward the bank in his 1959 Ford, his siren blasting and his red and blue lights turned on. Officer Davis had only been on the job for one month and had no real law enforcement experience. Before he'd taken the job as police officer he had worked in Oklahoma City for a local construction company. Officer Davis had yet to attend the mandatory training for Oklahoma's law enforcement officers; he had ninety days from his hire date to attend and become certified.

Entering the bank, the officer found himself shaking; he had never been involved in any investigation, let alone a bank robbery. As he walked in the bank, he did not wear gloves, and he failed to secure the crime scene. After ten minutes the bank president asked him if he was going to call the chief of police, Chief Joe Harwick.

"Sure I am," said Davis. Where is your phone?" Davis was given the phone and began to dial the number to the chief's residence. His fingers were trembling so badly he had to make three attempts before he was successful. "Chief, this is Davis. I thought you would want to know that the bank has been robbed." Davis's voice was full of anxiety and excitement, and he could barely talk. "Sure," said the officer after the chief's reply. "I will be here waiting for you."

Ten minutes later Chief Harwick arrived at the bank, driving without the lights or siren on in his 1960 pickup. He knew Officer Davis was on the scene, and besides, the citizens would already know about the robbery by now, so why provide more excitement than necessary? As the chief entered the bank, he took immediate control of the crime scene. He ordered Davis to get yellow crime scene tape and put it around the bank to keep onlookers away and then began to question the bank employees about what they had seen and heard and what the robbers had said to them. He asked if they had gotten a good look at the two men, how they were dressed, and if they had anything that seemed to be unusual, like scars.

The employees had little to offer; they had obeyed the orders of the robbers and kept their eyes looking down at the floor. They were able to say the two were white males, about five-foot-nine or maybe five-ten. The two were well-dressed, wearing gray suits, and the witnesses estimated the robbers to be in their mid-thirties. One of the employees said that when the robbers spoke they were "gruff" and very harsh with the words they used.

"Get a hold of the citizens who were in the bank and bring them to headquarters, I need to talk to them," Harwick instructed Davis. He knew they had left the bank as soon as they were untied and probably had gone home to the safe comfort of their residences.

After interviewing all the witnesses, Harwick called the FBI office in Oklahoma City to report the crime. The FBI had a branch that focused on bank robberies and had the experience to deal with this sort of crime. The agent who had taken the call said they were sending two field agents, Ronnie Ferguson and Steve Turner. The agent said the two would be there in the next two hours, and told Harwick, "Whatever you do, do not disturb the crime scene. This is important, okay?" Harwick told him the scene was secured but did not tell the agent the evidence may have been compromised when Officer Davis had first arrived on the scene. Harwick considered the case closed for his department, as the FBI had assumed jurisdiction.

As word spread through nearby towns like Glencoe, the news was considered interesting and made for good conversation, but other than that, it did not affect the citizens. The last robbery in Coyle had been in the 1800s, when the bank was robbed by the Doolin and Dalton gang, a notorious group of outlaws who were the first to rob two banks on the same day. The other victim was Coffeyville, Kansas. Also, the little town of Ingalls, located nearby, was a known hangout for desperados and the likes of Arkansas Tom. Bill Doolin and Bob Dalton were cousins to Frank and Jessie James of Missouri; crime ran in their blood. When their gang hit the Coyle bank, they made a clean getaway, and the money stolen was never recovered.

The town was quiet and peaceful when Doolin and his cohorts were there. The outlaw, Bill Doolin would come to Ingalls to see his wife, Edith, who worked at the Pierce Hotel and as a nurse to Dr. D. H. Self after her marriage to the outlaw ended. Ingalls was an isolated community and a safe refuge for the gang. The men would spend much of their time at the Bee Dunn ranch or the Sherm Sanders ranch not far away.

There had been one incident in the town when a group of young men attempted to break up a church meeting. Doolin and two of his gang, Roy Daugherty, alias Arkansas Tom, and George "Bitter Creek" Newcomb were present. All were wearing guns. Doolin finally stood up and said, "Go ahead, preacher, and preach. I'll keep order." And he did.

In the town of Ingalls they were treated as Robin Hoods, often giving cash to those in need. They spent a lot of money and never caused the people of Ingalls any problems. That is, until the United States Marshals from the territorial capital of Guthrie received word the gang was holed up in

Ingalls, and plans were made for their capture. The gang had just staged a double train robbery in Wharton, just north of Perry, Oklahoma, where the two trains stopped at the same time every day. The gang had then retreated to Ingalls.

During the last week in July, two informants arrived in Ingalls to study the outlaws' routine. On a Thursday night, August 31, 1893, two covered wagons carrying deputy US Marshals moved into town. Little attention was paid to them, as a constant stream of wagons had been passing through to make the Cherokee Strip run, just two weeks away. The next morning began with the usual business and serenity. Doolin and most of his gang were at the Ransom-Murray saloon. Arkansas Tom was feeling bad and still at the hotel. The marshals were planning their strategy.

Then, as Bitter Creek Newcomb casually led his horse down Ash Street, unaware of the marshals, a nervous deputy marshal fired, and the gunfight was under way. The marshals began firing at the saloon. Arkansas Tom punched a hole in the roof of the hotel and fired at the marshals. The people of Ingalls took cover while the gunplay went on. After only a few minutes of shooting, three marshals were shot. One, Richard Speed, died on the scene. Two others, Lafe Shadley and Tom Hueston, died later of their wounds. Two innocent bystanders were killed during the shooting, and two members of Doolin's gang were wounded, and as a result of the battle all but one of the criminals escaped.

Arkansas Tom was captured at the hotel. He was convicted and sent to prison after a trial in the frame courthouse in Stillwater. He was later released but died in a hail of bullets on August 16, 1924, in Joplin, Missouri, thirty-one years after the Ingalls gunfight. Doolin was killed on August 24, 1896, on the western edge of Lawson, later named Quay, located near Ingalls, while on a trip back to the area to pick up his wife and son.

In Glencoe, police officer Alan Downs had not taken any special precautions based on the Coyle robbery. He did not warn local businessmen or the local population to be on the lookout for strangers who might come to town. Coyle was thirty-six miles away and located near Interstate 35, close proximity to Oklahoma City, where a criminal could get lost in the crowd within thirty minutes of having committed a crime. Life in Glencoe had not changed, and there was no reason for it to; the crime had not affected the little town.

At the café the men met for coffee as they had done every day for the past three years. It was always at 7:00 a.m., when the café opened for business. The group discussed the robbery in Coyle and Panther sports. On this day they talked about the need for rain, as it had been a long summer and turned into a drought. As the men ordered coffee, Jean Stokes and Kay Murphy, co-owners of the café, pulled from the oven fresh-baked chocolate long john donuts.

The aroma spread through the air, and when offered one, each man said yes, he would like one to dip in his coffee.

As Bill Childers took his first bite, followed by a quick sip of coffee, Lynne Sawyer stepped in to order a BLT; she had not packed a lunch and did not want to eat in the cafeteria at school. While her sandwich was being wrapped, Barbara Ross came in to join her. Both girls were on the Lady Panthers basketball team, and both played the forward position. Before they left, the men asked how school was going, and as the girls started to answer, Frank Driskel said, "Just tell us how basketball practice is going." He laughed and then added, "We already know what kids think about school."

The girls said practice was going well, they thought they had a good team, and they were hoping for a good season. Once the girls were out the door, Frank said, "I hope they're right." The others at the table nodded in agreement.

Before the men had finished chatting, Andy Murphy dropped by and joined the group. He saw the long johns and ordered two for himself. Andy told the men he had been up since 4:00 a.m. tending to his watermelons. Sure enough, he was hot and sweaty. Andy always wore gray overalls and work boots. He told the men the drought had taken a toll on his crop, but with a little rain, he could salvage enough melons to still make a profit.

Each day the men would tune to Channel Nine in Oklahoma City to watch the weather. It didn't hurt that Ms. Lola Hall was the weather woman and gave the forecast every day at noon. Each forecast was to last for fifteen minutes, regardless of weather conditions. Lola was a tall blonde, slender, and had all her curves in the right places. Her smile brightened the television. Lola had not promised rain and during the summer months there had been little to report: hot, dry, and windy was the usual forecast, but because she had fifteen minutes airtime she would often talk about how the weather was affecting lakes in the area, and farmers.

Lola had a barrel as a prop that had the state of Oklahoma painted on it and the counties outlined in black. To see the U.S. map she would spin the barrel a third of the way around, position it directly in front of the camera, and point to any state she wanted to talk about. To get a world view she would again spin the map a third of a turn until the world view was visible.

The men began to laugh when one of them reminded the others how back in August Lola had gotten in trouble with her boss at the station and the federal boys when the news reporter had told the audience, "Stay tuned for the forecast, Lola has important information about the weather. The temperature is going to drop by fifteen degrees within the next twenty-four-hour period."

As the camera swirled over to Lola, she blurted out, "You son of a bitch, could you not wait for me to tell about it? The federal boys became involved and threatened to fine the station and demanded an apology. But Lola being Lola, she never gave in, and soon she was back in good graces with her boss.

After the story was told, each man laughed and one said, "Hell, we never watch to get the forecast. We can predict the weather as well as her, but not many women look as good as she does!" That day at noon Lola reported the weather to be hot, dry, and windy.

On television the first show to be broadcast in color was *Bonanza*. A star of the show was a character named Adam Cartwright, played by Pernell Roberts. The Cartwright character was smart, handsome, witty, and most importantly, he was single. A few years after the show first aired there were a rash of children born who were named Adam by their mothers.

In Glencoe, the only family in town that owned a color television set shortly after the series began was the Childers. Bill and Maxine Childers did not have any sons but had four lovely daughters. Linda, the second to the youngest, was tall, had red hair, played basketball, and enjoyed making friends. She enjoyed life, and once a week she would invite a different boy over to watch the popular show. The two of them would sit on the couch in front of the RCA twenty-eight-inch television, eat popcorn, and enjoy a soda. Linda had many boyfriends and enjoyed playing the field. In her junior year she was elected class personality, and in 1967 she was a contender to become basketball queen.

Carolyn Driskel and Linda Childers were friends, and the two of them would talk every night, the same time each night. Each had a princess telephone, but the colors were different. At school they would talk about basketball and boys they had dated or wanted to date, and they always made plans for the weekend. On the phone they would discuss important topics like who was dating who, who each of them should be dating, and what clothing purchases they had made recently. Carolyn had brown hair, brown eyes, and a special way with words. She could cut a boy to ribbons while sweet-talking him, and the boy never knew what had happened until he told someone what she'd said, who then would tell him how he had been criticized. Carolyn always had the last laugh.

As the men sat drinking coffee and eating their second donut each, pondering what Johnson was going to do about the war, civil rights, and the hippies, word came of a second bank robbery. This one was in Oklahoma City. The police were searching for two men, in their mid-thirties wearing gray suits, and both were white. The two had escaped without detection and had earned a good payday. No one in the bank had seen whether there was a getaway driver, and no one had seen the car they had escaped in. The FBI was called, and the agency joined together with the local cops to investigate. The Oklahoma City Police Department know how to handle a crime scene and how to investigate a crime of this magnitude. The FBI quickly put together a link between this bank robbery and the one in Coyle.

CHAPTER 6

Underdogs

THE PANTHER BASKETBALL TEAM had been practicing since the start of the school year, preparing for their first non-conference game. The pre-conference games provided an opportunity to prepare for the all important conference play, where the champions were crowned in January. Glencoe was in the Santa Fe Conference along with Ralston, Morrison, Kaw City, Marland, Red Rock, Burbank, and Ripley. Morrison was the powerhouse of the conference, having won the championship the last five straight years.

The Panthers' losing streak against the Tigers was long; they had not beaten them in ten years. But everyone thought this year would be different. The coach thought he had quality players and a will to win. The boys' team had all returning starters except for one, who had graduated the year before. The town's fans had heard rumors about how the team had been practicing, the hard work that was being put in, and everyone had seen the team players running daily during school days. The team would run to Linsenmeyer's corner and then run back to town, approximately four miles round trip. No one had ever seen conditioning like what was being demanded this year.

Bill Hodge, a tall center with blue eyes and blonde hair, was one of the favorites of the cheerleaders—and most importantly was not in a steady relationship, so he was fair game, thought the girls. Bill could shoot with accuracy while in the paint, and he could also rebound, make assists, and block shots. He was all muscle. Bill had been selected as an alternate all-conference player the year before, being nudged out of the first team selection by two points. Bill wanted a win badly against Morrison, as the previous year he had been embarrassed, being allowed only ten points and two rebounds when the two teams met in conference play. Bill blamed that game for his not having made the conference team.

John Clark was a returning starter and knew his role on the court; he was smart, quick as a cat, and could shoot from the top of the key. Bill and John made for a strong one-two punch. Assisting the two players were Dale Lyle, a lefty who was hard to hold down when on his game. Lyle had good range and always looked to find the open man before firing from long distance. Rounding out the team starters was Gary Mitchell, an impressive guard; and Larry Shell, short but a strong ball handler when bringing the ball down court as the team's point guard. The bench was considered strong, with Mike Wiseman, Larry Murphy, Randy Robinson, Keith Hodge, Eddie Porter, and Randy Clark.

The first game was scheduled to be played in two weeks against the Stillwater Pioneers' B-team. At the café, the Glencoe men talked about the team's chances against such a mighty opponent. Why would Coach Wallace schedule against a team that would likely beat the Panthers? they wondered. How would a defeat set the stage for the remainder of the year? The questions were asked, but none of the men had answers.

A town meeting was scheduled for 7:00 p.m. that evening at the Senior Citizens Center. Coach Wallace was the main speaker, and he would give the townspeople a preview of what was to come and would report on the progress of his team. At the end of the session, anyone wanting to ask a question would be allowed. Each week there would be another meeting at the same time and place, except because the basketball games were scheduled for Friday nights, the town meeting would be on Thursdays.

Before the meeting was to begin, the fans came to the Center to listen to Max Porter play his 1958 Fender guitar. He took requests and knew every song he was asked to play; those responsible for setting up the weekly meeting had done a good job assuring entertainment was part of the agenda.

During the meeting, Wallace provided a detailed description of how practice had been going for both the boys and girls teams. An injury update was provided, and so far the teams had no serious injuries, just a few bumps and bruises. The coach talked about the first opponent, Stillwater. He told the crowd that for the team to get better, the Panthers had to play quality opponents. "No more picking pre-conference games we know we will win," Wallace explained. "The goal of my Panthers team is to win the conference championship, and then from there—" he stopped and just smiled. Wallace said he had heard the rumors around town about playing Stillwater, how the people of the town thought it was a strategic mistake made by him, but he told them he did not agree. "We can beat the Pioneers," he said.

Wallace then announced he had an important announcement to make. "This year we have bought a video tape machine, and we will be able to tape all our games, critique our plays, examine the play of our players, and make adjustments during practice. This is a good purchase," said Wallace. "If my plans go right we will tape our opponents before we ever meet them on the court."

After Wallace finished, the people stood and began to applaud. Once the crowd quieted down, Wallace asked for a volunteer who was willing to tape each game, Loyal Honeyman stood and announced he was willing, able, and ready to assist the team. "Good," said Wallace, "you are our man."

After Loyal sat back down, Wallace told everyone in attendance he had a surprise for them. He then asked the cheerleaders and pom-pom girls to come to the front of the stage.

From the back of the building three cheerleaders came down the crowded aisle doing cartwheels. They landed near Wallace, who was standing by the cheap, fake-wood table where he had been seated for the question-and-answer part of the meeting. Once the girls landed they did three back flips while the three remaining cheerleaders came running, chanting, "Two, four, six, eight. Who do we appreciate?"

The crowd let out a loud yelp, "Panthers, Panthers that's our team! This year winning is our theme!"

While the crowd kept cheering and clapping, the pom-pom girls made their way to the front dressed, in their blue and gold, the team colors. Each girl had two pom-poms, one in each hand. The girls tossed the puffs into the crowd, where they were quickly given back. After a few minutes Wallace put his arms out as if to say, quiet down. Wallace then introduced each cheerleader and pom-pom girl.

"Give a big round of applause to Linda Childers, Brenda Ross, Kay Flowers, Carolyn Driskel, Linda Treat, Mary

Ann Shell, Cheryl Ryan, Becky Clark, Lynne Sawyer, and Marilyn Childers, these are your girl panthers who will bring home many wins this year," said Wallace. He then introduced the cheerleaders and pom-pom girls, "How about it folks," said Wallace, "here they are, Sandy Honeyman, Carlene Murphy, Marietta Cavett, Janine Chaffin, Andrea Shelton, Rhonda McGinty, and, Marsha Rossander. Following the introductions the crowd went to the girls and congratulated each and everyone for their commitment to the 'cause.'"

Before finishing for the night, Wallace told the crowd he demanded a lot from his players and expected perfection. "This is how we are going win, by playing perfect basketball," he said. He explained he wanted his forwards to be aggressive, look for good shots, make assists, rebound, and play together as a team. He then talked about the guards and his expectations of them for the year. Wallace wrapped up the meeting by saying he would introduce the boys' team players at the next meeting, one week away.

While Wallace was meeting with the townspeople, giving them updates on the progress of the team, the boys were at the gym shooting free throws, playing round robin, shooting from all corners of the court, and on occasion playing the game "Horse". Each player knew what was at stake, what it would take to make for a successful season rather than just a mediocre one. The players knew much of what was expected of them and committed to striving to be the best they could be; besides, they already had doubts about playing the Stillwater Pioneers' B-team.

As the players wrapped up practice, plans were made to meet in Stillwater afterward; the drag was waiting. Mike Crawford and Eddie Porter planned to meet at the Sonic, while Larry Shell was going to the drive-in with his steady, Christy Childers. Bill Hodge and John Clark were going on a double date; John was going out with Pam McCubbin, and Bill was to be with Carlene Murphy. Keith Hodge was picking up Rhonda McGinty at the Senior Citizens Center, and Lynne Sawyer was going on her first date with Mike Wiseman, a new guy in town who had started the new school year in Glencoe.

Chapter 7

Let the Game Begin

Between classes the next Monday, Marietta Cavetto and Becky Clark were walking in the hall, whispering to one another as they saw Porter approach. Becky put her hand to her mouth and started giggling. As they passed, Becky looked at Porter and shot him a smile. Marietta glanced at him and gave a quick wink, and then the two walked on.

Journalism class was beginning, and the class was to split into two teams to sell advertisements for the yearbook. Eddie Porter and Linda Lovell were the yearbook co-editors, and each would lead a team. Porter was to take five people and Lovell to take five. Each student was asked if they preferred going to Pawnee or Stillwater. Donna Cronk, Wesley Fritchman, Vickie Beverage, and Carolyn Driskel volunteered to go to Pawnee. They became part of Porter's team.

Marietta arrived late to class and when learning the class was being split into separate teams she went to Ms. Murphy and requested to be a part of Porter's team. As the team prepared to leave town to go to Pawnee, Marietta and Donna climbed in the front seat of Porter's car, which was equipped with bucket seats. Marietta was close to being on Porter's lap. When they entered Pawnee, they stopped for a coke and to plan their strategy on which businesses to approach and how the team should be split. Marietta suggested they work in teams of two, then saying she would partner with Porter. Before the three teams hit the street, they agreed to meet back at the car at noon.

Bonnas Warden, in journalism class, had heard Marietta say she wanted to go with Porter. When he had heard her say his name, he tensed up and become red-faced but had not said a word.

Back at the high school, Deputy Russell returned, parking his LTD in front of the school. When he entered the building, he went directly to Superintendent Howard's office and closed the door. He told Howard that although he was convinced he knew who had committed the vandalism, he was unable to prove it. He said he wanted to continue the investigation, but the sheriff told him he was being pulled off the case; the sheriff needed him on other cases.

After the deputy left, Howard sat down on his desk chair, reached over, got a white piece of paper, and began to write. After he finished, he went to see the students. He told them he knew who the criminals were but had decided not to pursue the investigation any further, since the school had not experienced any new incidents in the past year. Howard did not tell them the deputy had been pulled off the case; he needed to save face. As Howard turned to walk out the door, he told the students he had meant business and was sure they knew it by now.

Once the door closed behind him, Larry Shell looked to his right at Mike Phillips and then to his left at Max Haken. Each grinned, and then the three of them looked straight ahead at the teacher, who was writing on the blackboard. The three knew they had gotten away with the prank and were thankful Howard had decided to abandon the investigation.

During the rest of the day, between classes, the girls talked about the fun they had had at the Senior Citizens Center, what they had done afterward, who they had gone on a date with, and what they wanted to do next weekend. The boys talked about having a party the following weekend, maybe in Stillwater, Yost Lake, or someplace else.

As the players prepared for the game against the Pioneers, the townspeople were anxious for the season to get started. The girls always played the first game while the boys waited for them to finish. The bleachers were full of students and fans; there was a standing-room-only crowd, all of whom were in a good mood. The time had finally arrived. During the pregame warm-ups the girls were shooting well, the guards were practicing their moves against other guards, and they moved quick and seemed to anticipate well—but again, they were only warming up against their own teammates. They knew each others' moves.

On the other end of the court the Pioneer ladies were running drills, including layups and shots from the corners. They appeared to be on target, and they also seemed confident. After the warm-ups were finished, both teams huddled around their respective coaches. Wallace gave his final instructions before tip-off. He told his girls to play with confidence, to keep their heads in the game and stay focused. He reminded the guards to be aggressive but also be smart.

As Lynne Sawyer entered the circle to jump for Glencoe, she was met by Nelda Alley, a six-foot-two forward who stood five inches taller than Lynne. Lynne gave a quick look to Carolyn, who knew she would have to be aggressive to get to the ball. When the referee tossed the ball in the air, it was tipped to the Stillwater Pioneers. Carolyn had anticipated where the ball would go; she moved to the forward who caught the ball while waving her arms. The forward bounce passed the ball back to Nelda. Carolyn moved to guard Nelda and within seconds had stolen the ball from the Pioneer starter.

Carolyn dribbled to center court and then passed off to Linda Childers, who saw an opening and drove to the bucket. But as she entered the paint, two defenders came toward her preventing her from advancing any farther. Linda and her teammates had played together long enough that she knew where they would be stationed on the court. As soon as she saw the two defenders, she tossed the ball back over her head and into the arms of Lynne at the free throw line with an uncontested shot. She took aim, shot, and hit, all net. Glencoe was up two to nothing.

As the Pioneers inbounded the ball they received little pressure from the Lady Panther guards and were able to move the ball easily to center court, where it was passed to Nelda. Nelda recognized the guards in a man-to-man defense; she had given up a turnover the last time and had no intention of making the same mistake again. As she scouted the floor, she saw one of the other forwards in the corner. The defense was playing loose, so she passed off to her teammate and then moved into the paint. It was a play the Pioneers had used before; Nelda was open, and the ball came quickly back to her for an easy lay-up. As the game continued the lead switched back and forth several times. At halftime the Panthers trailed by two points.

The crowded gym was full of spirit and excitement at the beginning of the second half. The fans cheered at every play made by the Panthers, and the girls knew they had the support of a friendly crowd, but they had to figure out a way to stop the Lady Pioneers. At halftime Coach Wallace had told the guards to begin applying pressure. "Don't let them have a free walk to center court," he said. "If they have the freedom to maneuver, we will be dead in the water." "Make sure Alley is covered, she is killing us," said Wallace.

Carolyn and the other guards took the words seriously. Kay Flowers and Linda Treat knew they had to step up their game. As the second half began, the Panthers were handed the ball by the referee since they had been out-jumped in the first half. Childers inbounded to Brenda Ross, who passed off to Lynne Sawyer. The girls kept the ball in motion, trying to wear down the opposing guards. With just six seconds left on the shot clock Brenda saw an opening; the opposing guards had expected her to drive the ball, but when she started toward the basket, Lynne broke free, and Brenda passed to her in the corner, where Lynne nailed the open jumper.

The game was now tied, and the pressure was on the Panther guards. Nelda had the ball for the Pioneers; she had scored twelve points in the first half and was looking to add to her total. Carolyn moved toward Nelda to apply additional pressure and to take away her long shot. It worked; as Nelda attempted to go around Carolyn, Kay Flowers planted herself just to Nelda's right, and the tall Pioneer ran into her and was called for charging. The turnover gave the Panthers the opportunity to score and take the lead.

As in the first half, the score kept going back and forth for much of the second; Nelda continued to get her shots and added to her total until the final two minutes of the game. Then the Glencoe girls switched from man-to-man to a zone defense. The paint would be guarded at all times, so if the Pioneers wanted to score, they had to shoot long range—shots considered to be low percentage. As the Panthers maintained a two-point lead late the Pioneers became frustrated. They had to make a play to even the score with thirty seconds left on the clock.

The ball was inbounded to Nelda, and she would not relinquish it and would wait until there were just five seconds on the clock to make her play. As the clock wound down, she drove to the basket, put up the shot while in the air, and was fouled. Her shot did not score, but she had two free throws coming. If she could make them both it would be a tie game, and they would play a five-minute overtime.

As Nelda stood at the line, she took a deep breath, and she made the first shot with ease. Before she let go with her second shot, Wallace called time-out. He told his girls to get the rebound in case she missed and to make sure they did not foul if they couldn't get the rebound. "Don't foul, don't foul," Wallace repeated. The coach was also hoping the time-out would freeze Nelda, give her time to think about the shot, and if all went well, the Panthers would escape by the skin of their teeth.

Nelda stood back at the free throw line. She bounced the ball two times, took a deep breath, and then shot. The ball went into the cylinder and kept spinning around the iron, and only after what seemed like an eternity did it roll out. Carolyn was in the right place at just the right time; she retrieved the rebound and held the ball until the buzzer went off; the Panthers then left the floor to a thunderous standing ovation by the fans.

The cheerleaders and pom-pom girls quickly changed into their uniforms and took their positions near the goal against the wall. The girls had beaten an opponent most people thought they could not beat; the girls were full of energy and ready to support the boys.

As the buzzer sounded to start the second game of the double-header, Larry Shell pulled the team together in the center of the court. He told them now was their time, that if they played together as a team and executed the plays, they would win the game. As he finished, the five starters shouted in unison, "Panthers!"

Glencoe took immediate control at the tip-off, and Shell dribbled down court with little pressure. The Pioneers were playing a zone defense, and Shell knew that tossing the ball into the paint would cause the Pioneers to collapse on the player with the ball, making it difficult to score under the basket. Fortunately, Mike Wiseman had an eagle eye and had been hitting from all over the court in practice.

Shell threw the ball into the paint to Bill Hodge, who saw Wiseman and kicked the ball to him in the corner. Wiseman took the shot and scored.

As the Pioneers took possession, they began to drive down the court. Shell applied pressure, as did Gary Mitchell in a full-court press. The Pioneers tossed the ball around in an attempt to slow the tempo down; knowing Glencoe liked a fast-paced game. The Pioneers found an opening and took a shot but missed; John Clark rebounded and threw downcourt to Shell, who had moved back in the event the Panthers were able to get the rebound. As Shell grabbed the ball in air, he took one step and made an easy layup. The Panthers were leading by four in the early minutes of the game.

By the second half the team had stretched its lead to ten; it seemed easy, thought the starters and their coach. Near the end of the fourth quarter, the Panthers had extended their lead to eighteen points. "Time to put in the subs," said Coach Wallace during a planned time-out. "Porter, you replace Shell. Crawford, you take Mitchell's spot. Keith, you go in for Lyle. Robinson, you're in for Wiseman. And Clark, I want you in for Bill."

As the last two minutes ticked off the clock, the Panthers extended their lead by another four points. The subs played well, Coach Wallace was pleased at the end of the game, and all the Panthers would celebrate along with the fans that had come out to support them.

CHAPTER 8

The Hunt Begins

T HE FBI AND OKLAHOMA City Police Department had interviewed all witnesses who had been taken hostage by the robbers and interviewed everyone in a two-block area. No one had seen anyone suspicious. From the little information the two agencies had, they made a decision to send all that was known to the Behavioral Analysis Unit at the FBI headquarters in Virginia and let the profile boys take a hard look at the data. The agents described the scene as they found it but had little else to offer. They were hoping the profilers would come up with something to help them with the investigation and give them an idea of the type of person who would commit such a daring crime.

In the meantime, all banks in the Oklahoma City metro area and in a fifty-mile radius had quietly been told to be cautious, as they could be the next target of the robbers. The FBI did know a pattern had been established thanks to the Coyle holdup; the two suspects always wore gray suits, robbed during daylight hours, and took hostages who were always tied up. The most important information they gathered was that the robbers seemed likely to be violent if tho folt cornered.

As the manhunt intensified, the robbers were holed up in a sleazy motel just outside Oklahoma City in the town of Guthrie. Guthrie was located on Interstate 35 and was a quiet town where most locals knew one another; however, because it was a town that had many strangers who exited off the interstate highway to eat a meal, fill up their cars, or to find a hotel in which to spend the night the robbers thought they would go undetected. To make sure they kept a low profile they ordered meals to be served in their room. The two paid with cash, avoiding the use of credit cards, which would be traced. The two were organized, and before each bank robbery they had scouted the town and the bank, looking for video cameras, and they knew the size of the town's police force.

So far the robbers' luck had held. They knew the FBI and the Oklahoma City Police Department had little information on them—at least, the newspapers and news networks had reported nothing new. As the robbers sat in their motel room they began to plan their next strike. They had not hit a bank in three weeks and felt their next robbery would be another successful one as long as they did their homework and planned well.

The two sat on one of two beds in the room and unfurled a state map. After they spread the map on the bed, they used pushpins to show each bank they had scouted, which banks they had already hit, and which were lower risk than others. The robbers did not know exactly what action the FBI had taken to alert other banks but knew they must have done something; the question they pondered was, what was the radius of alert they had set up?

The robbers decided it was too risky to rob another bank in the same vicinity as the first two. As they continued to debate the best location for their next job, scanning the map, suddenly one of the men pointed to Glencoe, a small town which had already been scouted. The town had one police officer, whom they referred to as Barney Fife. They knew the bank had deposits from local ranchers, farmers, business owners, and a few people in other towns. The two would not have considered the bank at all except they had read that it was also being used as a depository for several Indian tribes who had won a federal lawsuit over the dispute of native lands.

The Sac and Fox, Ponca, Pawnee, and Iowa tribes had been awarded millions of dollars. The tribes had a choice where to deposit the money, if at all. Knowing the money could provide a considerable amount of interest for them to use to pursue other business ventures, the tribal leaders had chosen to invest it. The tribes in Oklahoma had recently begun to create smoke shops, hotels, casinos, and other profitable businesses as they increased their tribal incomes. Before each tribe decided where to put their money, they met with bankers across the state and region to negotiate interest rates on the money. Most banks were so excited about the prospect of receiving millions of dollars that they eagerly agreed to add one interest point for every million deposited.

The Glencoe State Bank had made a good offer, and several tribes had decided to deposit considerable amounts in the bank. Clarence McGinty had a long history with the tribal leaders and had always treated the natives with respect; there was a trusting bond between McGinty and the tribal leaders, which had helped the tribal leaders, make the decision to deposit their money in the Glencoe State Bank.

Glencoe Bank in 2011

When Eddie Porter and Mike Crawford met at the Stillwater Sonic, they decided to drive to the A&W located at the end of the drag. Once they got there, Mike parked his car and then got into Porter's. As the two made the drag between the Sonic and A&W, Porter put in a Johnny Rivers 8-track tape, and they began to listen to "Maybellene." They turned the volume up and rolled the windows down; they wanted to be heard as well as seen. As they cruised, they would honk their horn at cars they knew, and the others would honk back, a signal to say hello. Throughout the night, regardless of how many times the cars had already honked, they would keep up the ritual until they went home.

After dragging for a couple of hours, the two decided to go back to the A&W, park, and sit on the hoods of their cars and wait for others to come driving through. They had not been there long when Max Haken and his girlfriend, Rhonda Nichols, came through the parking lot. The couple said they had just arrived in town and wanted to know where the party was. As they were talking, David Horner and Lorraine Roper came cruising by slowly.

"Hey, Barbwire," yelled Mike. "Where is your motorcycle?" Mike and the others started laughing at the comment. David had been given the nickname "Barbwire" after one night, having had too much to drink; he'd driven his motorcycle into a farmer's barbwire fence. He hadn't been seriously injured but did now have scars on both knees to prove his toughness.

Carrie Robinson, Brenda Jones, and Marsha Rossander came by looking for boys—not any particular boy, just boys. Brenda had a boyfriend who lived in Tulsa. The two had been dating for the past three months; he drove a

Jaguar and made the trip to Glencoe every weekend since they had begun their relationship. But for this weekend, he had called her earlier in the day and said he would be unable to make it; he had to go out of town on a family trip with his parents and younger brother.

Brenda joked that since she was free she was going to make the most of it. Brenda had a reputation she needed to keep intact. Marsha and Carrie were innocent girls who were along for the ride; besides, they could meet someone nice and have some fun of their own for a couple of hours. Brenda had the experience and knew how to ditch her two friends if things began to go her way. As the girls continued to circle the parking lot, Brenda shouted that they were headed to the strip located near the OSU campus; there would be action there.

Bonnas Warden drove a blue Cushman motorcycle. It was known to be a fast machine; it had an automatic transmission that shifted gears with ease. When riding, Warden always wore a leather jacket with the collar pulled up. He would not wear a helmet and always wore tight jeans with a white T-shirt. Warden had not dated anyone for months but had his eye on Marietta Cavett; unfortunately for him, she did not have eyes for him. As he came through the A&W parking lot, he slowed down and came to a stop. He remained on the bike and asked if anyone had seen Marietta. The group said they had not, and as he was driving off, he yelled, "If you see her, tell her I'm looking for her."

After another hour of sitting in the parking lot, Mike and Porter decided to make a run to the strip. When they arrived they saw a mixture of college students and the "Glencoe gang." Brenda had found a guy, and they had gone behind one of the local businesses for some "private time." Marsha and Carrie were drinking a soda and talking about how they would get home. They had ridden into Stillwater with Brenda, and their cars were parked on Main Street back in Glencoe. They knew they would be ready to leave before Brenda.

Warden was still cruising around looking for Marietta. Max and Rhonda were nowhere in sight. After parking, Mike and Porter went to the Hideaway Pizza Parlor, a popular spot for college students, as the Hideaway had the best pizza in town. As they started toward the parlor, they saw Marsha and Carrie and asked the girls if they wanted to join them. The ladies agreed, and they entered the pizza parlor and found a booth, ordering a large pepperoni pizza and a pitcher of Coke.

As they ate and talked about their night, the girls asked if they could hitch a ride back to Glencoe. "Sure," said the boys, "we will be leaving in about an hour; you can hang with us until we leave." The girls agreed.

At midnight the four left and went back to the A&W, where Porter had parked his '63 Ford Galaxy. The car had black leather seats, a black vinyl top, automatic transmission on the floor, and red and white lights in the door. As Porter got out of Mike's car, Marsha said she would ride with him, and Carrie would go back with Mike. The two cars headed out, and they made the drag between the Sonic and the A&W one last time. They did not pass or see anyone they knew, so they simply drove to the intersection of Highway 51 and Main, where they turned left, the way back to Glencoe. As they drove into the small town, each parked next to four cars already parked on Main Street. The girls got out, went to their cars, and left for the evening.

After ten minutes Marietta drove up; she had been to a movie with one of her many friends and was ready to meet up with the guys who were back in town. As soon as she drove up, Mike told her that Warden had been looking for her. When hearing this she rolled her eyes and said with emphasis, "I am not going to go out with him, *ever*."

Marietta then said she was not ready to go home; it was 12:30 a.m., and she said she did not need to be home until one. She then approached Porter and said, "Let's take a ride."

As the two drove off, Warden came roaring up on his bike. He again asked if anyone had seen Marietta, and the group told him no; they were not about to say she and Porter had just left together. Warden then parked his motorcycle alongside the parked cars. The rest of the group told Warden they were leaving in hopes he would leave as well.

Just as they were getting into their cars about to leave, Marietta and Porter came back. Warden saw the two together and went to Porter, who told him he had just run into Marietta, and she'd mentioned she thought her car was acting up. "I went with her to see if the car is having a problem," Porter said.

Warden did not go for it, and he was pissed. As Porter was walking away, Warden charged toward him, but Mike grabbed Warden and told Marietta to leave. Without a word she got in her car, started it, and peeled off. Mike told Porter to leave as well, but before he could get to his car, Warden broke away from Mike, went to his motorcycle saddle bags, and grabbed a lug wrench. He told Porter he was going to beat him to a pulp.

Porter tried to talk to him, saying it was not what it looked like and he would never move in on a girl Warden was trying to hook up with. As Warden approached with the lug wrench in hand. Mike grabbed Warden once again, and this time others present jumped in and took hold of the angry bike rider. They told Porter to leave, and this time he made it to his car while Warden was still being held in bondage.

As Porter was driving off, Warden shouted out, "This is not over!" Once Porter was out of sight, the boys let Warden go. He went to his bike, started it, and drove away while thinking, *I will settle this another day.*

CHAPTER 9

Celebration and Conflict

THE CROWD RUSHED THE floor; the Boy Panthers had beaten the Pioneers. This was not supposed to happen. In years past, it never would have, but this was a new year with a new dedication by the players and coach. The boys and girls Panther teams were better than in years past, plus they were well coached, in excellent physical condition, had a game plan that they followed, and they had the spirit to win.

As the coach was congratulating his players, he saw Loyal Honeyman, the video cameraman. As Wallace approached Honeyman hands were extended to the coach by fans that had come on the court to congratulate the players. When Wallace eventually got to Honeyman, he asked if the tape would be ready for Monday's practice. Honeyman assured him it would be and then slapped the coach on the back and left.

Wallace was smiling as his players hoisted their coach in the air and began carrying him around the court. After parading around the perimeter two times he was gently let back down to the floor. Wallace let the players celebrate for an additional few minutes and then told them to go to the locker room; he knew he could not afford for any of the team members to become injured in the fracas. The fans began to leave the school, and the players heard the cars honking as they drove away.

As the boys and girls exited the locker room, they were met by Wallace. He told them he was proud of their efforts during the game, how well they had practiced, and how well they'd played their game. He then issued a warning: "Don't let this victory go to your head, it is just one game. We have plenty of improvements to make. I will see you at practice on Monday."

Pawnee had played Yale while Glencoe took on the Pioneers; Pawnee was the defending Class A state champions and looked to repeat. In their game with Yale they had easily dominated, running the ball up and down the court, playing stellar defense, and shooting a sizzling 62 percent from the floor. The game was a warm-up, thought the players, and was the first step to repeating their championship status. The Black Bears knew their next opponent would be Glencoe, but they had no concerns about the little town—just another Yale, they thought. An easy victory lay ahead.

As the Panthers left the gym, they arranged to meet on Main Street to plan the rest of the evening. It was 10:30 p.m., and each knew they did not have long to decide before they would need to go home to comply with their curfew. The players knew going to Stillwater was out; the Pioneers would not be in a good frame of mind, and why rub it in their faces thought the Panthers. As they pondered where to go and what to do, someone suggested Pawnee; it was a mere fourteen miles away and was their next opponent. So it was decided, Pawnee it would be; besides, they wanted to send a message to the Bears that they would be in for a fight. Pawnee had heard of the Panther victory, and the players thought they could give them a friendly hello while in town.

As the cars were lining up to go to Pawnee, Warden drove up in his light-blue mustang, having decided not to drive the Cushman motorcycle. Warden had purchased the Mustang used but it was without a scratch or dent. It had a 302 engine and could really move when pressed.

Porter was in his car in the procession line when Warden pulled next to him and said through his window, "Porter, this is not over."

Porter looked at Warden and said, "There is no business to take care of, Bonnas."

Warden did not move. He told Porter he would get him when the time is right, Porter looked in the eyes of Warden and said, "You need to grow up." The procession began to move, and Porter drove on.

In Guthrie, the bank robbers had decided since it had been three weeks since their last robbery, they were ready to strike again, and they had settled on Glencoe. The robbery was planned for the following week. To change their pattern, they decided to strike late at night, when the townspeople would be sleeping; there would be no hostages and no one around to identify them. The two had given careful consideration to changing the way they robbed banks; they did not want to give the FBI any clues they were the same men who had robbed the Coyle and Oklahoma City banks. They decided to take a look at the town and the bank one more time before the robbery.

Four cars led the procession to Pawnee. In the lead car were Keith and his date, Rhonda, with Linda Childers, Mary Ann Shell, and Becky Clark in the backseat. Following behind was Max Haken with his steady, Rhonda Nichols. With them were Ginger Harting, Carolyn Driskel, and Kay Flowers. The third car was driven by Kelly Murphy; he had just bought new silver Camaro. Kelly had begun to date Donna, and she rode with him in the front seat, while Linda Treat and Randy Clark occupied the backseat. The car bringing up the rear was Eddie Porter, and with him were Don Sosbee, a kid from Wewoka who had come to meet up with Porter and to party, as well as Andrea Shelton, Lynne Sawyer, Sandy Honeyman, and Jeff Stevens. Porter's 1963 Galaxy was packed with people in the back, sitting practically on each other.

As the group entered Pawnee at 11:00 p.m., they drove through town down Main Street. The Bears had finished their game and were cruising the street, honking and having a good time. When the Pawnee players began to recognize the strangers cruising their drag were from Glencoe, they began to shout insults to the Panthers. The Panthers were not looking for trouble, and a quick decision was made to leave the main drag and to go to Pawnee Lake, where they could park and talk.

Within minutes of their arrival, a pickup rolled up with a bed full of Black Bear players. As the pickup unloaded, the boys stepped toward the Panthers. "This is our spot," said one of the Bears, "so why don't you pack up and get out? We don't need scum like you around here."

As the player finished, Keith stepped forward and told the aggressors they had not come for trouble, but the parking lot looked to him like it was big enough for the Panthers and Bears to both be there. He then told them they would be staying.

Bears players began taking off their coats. Just at that moment, Leland Ross and his wife, Brenda, drove up in his four-by-four pickup. Leland stood six-foot-two and was all muscle, not someone a person would want to tangle with. He got out of his pickup and walked over to Keith, asking if there was a problem. At the same time Max came rolling in, got out, walked to a Pawnee player, and put his finger on the player's chest and said, "There is no problem, isn't that right?"

The Pawnee players knew the reputations of both Max and Leland and did not want any part of what these two could dish out. The players got back in their pickup and sped away, tossing gravel from the tires as they peeled out. As they were leaving, one of them shouted, "We will whip your asses on the court. Don't be late!"

Sosbee hollered back, "Here I am, why wait?"

Once the parade of cars reentered Glencoe they parked, tuned their radios to KOMA 1520 AM, and turned up the volume. The station was playing "Proud Mary," and then the dancing began. The Panthers had beaten a team thought by the fans to be unbeatable. As they continued celebrating, other cars came and parked alongside them. Becky Clark's boyfriend drove up, and when seeing her took her in his arms, lifted her in the air, and planted a kiss on her lips. Rhonda and Keith started to do the twist when the station started playing "Twist and Shout" by the Beatles. Lynne Sawyer, Mike Wiseman, and Brenda and Leland Ross were there, and Leland was slapped on the back by the participants for his heroism just an hour earlier. Max and Rhonda came driving into town, parked, got out of their car, and joined the dance group. Fifteen minutes later, John Clark and Pam McCubbin came driving up but would not say where they had been. Linda Treat and Kay Flowers came into town; Kay was looking for Luke Driskel, while Linda was hunting Charles Robinson.

As the music played and the dancing continued, the teenagers saw headlights moving slowly down Main but could not identify the car because of the lights shining in their eyes. As the car came closer they noticed it was Coach Wallace, driving home to his single-wide trailer located at the end of Main Street, just beyond the U-turn. As Wallace passed by, he began to slow down and then backed up. With his window down and his arm on the window seal, he asked where everyone had been and told them they needed to go home.

Keith walked over to his car and explained, "Coach we have been to Pawnee, and you will never believe what happened."

At that time Wallace's smile faded away and a frown quickly replaced it. He pointed his finger toward Keith and then pushed it forward to where it was in his chest. "Are you crazy?" he said. "Don't you know what is going to happen now?" Wallace then got out of his car and went to where the others were standing. "What do you think you're doing, are you stupid? Do you think they need any more motivation than what they already have?" Wallace was walking back and forth as he spoke; he had lost his swagger and was clearly furious. "I want all of you to go home; you just made my job and yours harder." Wallace then returned to his car and drove away. As he got to his trailer, the teens could hear the front door of the trailer slam shut.

Two days later, Wallace met with the townspeople at the Senior Citizens Center. As he approached the fake wooden table, the crowd stood, applauded, and shouted congratulatory statements. Wallace thanked the crowd and then sat down. He told the crowd he was proud of the Panther teams he had coached against the Pioneers. "They're tough," he said. "They have talent and skill; my job is to get them in the right frame of mind, give them a workable game plan, and then let them play." He told the crowd he had expected a tough game with the Pioneers and said he was not disappointed. "I predicted a win," he reminded the crowd, rising to his feet. "I'd heard the rumors, how we couldn't beat the Pioneers, what it would mean to our season with an opening loss. But again, we have a good team that can go far this year. Even so, we will be underdogs in several of our games; I want you to remember that. I am not saying we will lose—we won't if I have anything to say about it." He then sat back down.

Wallace told the crowd the next opponent was Pawnee and reminded everyone, "Now the Black Bears are the defending Class A state champions. They want to repeat, and we are just one more team that stands in their way." Then he thanked Loyal Honeyman for having taped the Pioneer game and said he was already finding it useful. "I have found some mistakes we should not have made," he said, "and I have reviewed the tape given to me by the Yale coach, which shows their strengths and weaknesses. Pawnee will be tougher and harder to beat than the Pioneers were. They are a good—no, they are a great team. They have speed, depth, and all their players are back from their championship team. But they *are* beatable, and we are the team that will give them their first loss of the year." The crowd went wild with excitement; Coach Wallace had said they were beatable, good news to the listeners' ears.

The following day at the end of practice Wallace called for his players to sit on the bench while he talked. Wallace began by saying he was proud of the players and how they had performed against the Pioneers, and then he said, "But I am disappointed you let the victory go to your heads. You had no business going to Pawnee, and now they will be waiting for us."

He told the players practice was going to be tougher than in the past. As the players listened, they were thinking, how could it get any tougher than it already has been? Wallace continued, "I expect a lot from each and every one of you. If you think you can't work any harder than you already have, then I hate to disappoint you, but you can and will. I have a game plan," he said. "Tomorrow we will begin to implement it and work out the bugs." He finished and dismissed the players, telling them to be prepared for tomorrow's practice.

Porter left the school and headed for his car. Just as he began to open the driver's door he was surprised by Warden and caught a left hook to the jaw, knocking him to the ground. Porter grabbed his jaw. *Not broken*, he thought to himself. *Lucky me*. He then proceeded to tell Warden he would not fight him. "I have done nothing wrong," he said.

Warden responded, "You are trying to get my girl."

Just as Warden was threatening to attack Porter once again, Mike Phillips appeared, saw what had happened and made his way to the scene. "What are you doing?" asked Phillips to Warden. "Are you crazy, keep this up and you will be expelled."

Warden looked at Phillips, took a swing but missed as Phillips moved his head back. As Warden was off balance Phillips threw a right cross knocking Warden to the ground.

Before Porter even got off the ground he asked, "Are you finished?" Warden just stared at him and then spat on the ground after he had gathered his senses following the blow by Phillips. Warden barely missed Porter's head, and then he looked at Phillips and said, "This is none of your business, stay out of it." Phillips clearly had gotten the better of Warden and responded with, "You made it my business when you took a swing at me." Warden then got into his Mustang and peeled out the parking lot. Porter thought, *Maybe this thing will never be over.*

At school the next day, Jack Pritchard, the Vocational Agricultural teacher, announced the date for the annual Future Farmers of America banquet. He told the chapter members the banquet would be held in two weeks on a Wednesday night, and he explained that the members needed to select a Sweetheart Queen. He told them they would first take nominations for the queen and then vote on the girls nominated.

Porter was president of the chapter and by tradition would be the person to crown the queen at the banquet. Max Haken was another member, and when his girlfriend's name came up, he froze, his muscles beginning to tense up. He felt he was in a bind; on one hand, she should be queen. On the other, she would be kissed by the president, Porter.

After the nominations had been made, Pritchard said it was time for the vote. When Rhonda's name came up, she received ten of the fourteen votes. "It's settled," said Pritchard. "The new queen is Rhonda Nichols."

When the bell rang signaling time to change classes, Max walked over to Porter and punched him hard in the arm. Max had sent a message; he did not like the idea of someone other than himself kissing his girlfriend. Porter knew what the punch had meant. *It will be a long two weeks*, thought Porter. *I will be lucky if I am not in the hospital by the time the banquet gets here. Now I have Warden and Max to watch out for.*

On Friday night the United Methodist Church was hosting a hayrack ride where there was a bonfire, hot dogs, sodas, and chips. Everyone was invited to attend, and they met at the church at 7:00 p.m. and then hopped on the trailer loaded with straw, pulled by a powerful John Deere tractor. The destination was the Dewitt farm, where the bonfire had been prepared in a wooded area.

Marietta and Warden were on their first date, even though Marietta had declared it would never happen. They were sitting near the front of the trailer as it pulled away, their legs hanging down off the side of the trailer. Once they all reached the Dewitt farm, the bonfire was lit, and everyone began to move around the fire. Some got sticks and began to roast weenies and marshmallows; others continued to sit on the trailer, talking.

Warden had cooled down toward Porter and was beginning to warm up. Porter saw them together and thought, *Maybe he is okay now that he has a date with her. He should know by now that I have not tried to move in on her.*

Warden soon climbed off the trailer to fix a hot dog for his date and to get her a soothing drink. As soon as he left toward the bonfire and was a good thirty feet from the trailer and out of sight of everyone, Marietta went to the back, where Porter and Phillips sat. "Come with me," she said, taking Porter's hand. "I have something to tell you and I need to do it in private."

Porter knew it was risky; he had just started feeling like he could be around Warden and not take a licking. But he went anyway. Marietta led the way to a crop of trees well away from the bonfire. As they reached the trees, she spun around and put her arms around Porter's shoulders and then kissed him.

Wow, thought Porter, *I was not expecting that*. Porter considered Marietta a friend but not a girl he wanted to date. How could he explain this? He said nothing about the kiss but told Marietta they needed to get back to the camp. As they walked back, all he could think of was that he needed to not say a word to anyone about what had just happened, to just mingle with the crowd as if nothing had occurred, and most importantly, to stay away from Marietta. When they arrived, Marietta resumed her place near the front of the trailer, and Porter went to the bonfire and started a conversation with Phillips.

Phillips asked what Marietta had wanted, and all Porter could think to tell him was, "She just wanted to thank me for being her friend and to apologize for the jaw incident when Bonnas hit me." Phillips was satisfied, and the subject was not raised again that night.

On the way back to town after leaving the weenie roast, Porter noticed that Warden and Marietta were not talking, that something seemed wrong. Porter began to think back to when Warden had first transferred to Glencoe Elementary School. On his first day of class, Ms. Kincaid, the third grade teacher, had the students sitting in a circle. She said that each student would read a paragraph and then it was time for another to read, and this would go on until a chapter had been read. As Porter had finished his assigned paragraph it was Warden's turn; he had sat down by Porter, and at the time Warden did not know any of the students.

Ms. Kincaid asked Warden to read, but he just sat there staring at the book. Porter looked over and noticed he had his book turned upside down, so he reached over and turned it to its proper position. Warden then began to read, but he was not at the same level as the other students, though he would soon catch up.

Now, as Porter tried to figure out why Marietta and Warden were not talking, he kept thinking that someone must have seen her with Porter and told Warden. *Just my luck*, said the voice in his head that had begun speaking to him. *An innocent kiss with a girl I don't want to date is going to be the death of me yet.*

After the trailer arrived back at the church, everyone was ready to go home; they had school the next day, and the players on the basketball team had one of their stepped up, grueling practices to look forward to. Warden and Marietta were still not talking except for a few occasional words. As the two got off the trailer, they went to the blue Mustang and drove off, Warden taking Marietta home. She lived just a couple of miles outside of town, and Warden could go straight home from there, as her house was on his way.

Before everyone had left the church Warden had returned; he was looking for Porter, who was still in town talking with some of his friends. Warden pulled up violently and came to a screeching halt, put his car in park and then went to his trunk, where he got a lug wrench. He had the attention of everyone present by the way he had come to a stop.

"I am going to kill you!" he shouted to Porter, out of control.

Four of the guys present went over to him and asked what was wrong. Warden just stared at Porter and then moved toward him with the lug wrench in hand. Once the four saw that Warden was out of control, they moved quickly to subdue him; they wrapped their arms around him and told Porter to leave. Warden then blurted out that Marietta had told him, when taking her home, "She does not want to date me; she said she wants to date you."

Porter tried to find the right words. "I can't control what she thinks," he said. "Anyway, she is not my type."

"Porter, leave," said Larry Shell. "Go now."

As Porter left, he thought to himself, *Another close one. This thing needs to get settled. Now I am going to be killed just because some girl wants to date me . . .*

Instead of going straight home Porter decided to drive around for a while; he was too wound up to settle down. After driving around for an hour, he was ready to go home, but first he took one more drag down Main. Heading east on Main, he approached the stop sign at Highway 108, the road that would take him home.

Another car was driving slowly down 108 with its signal light on, turning onto Main. The men did not look familiar to Porter, but then, it was pitch dark and hard to see the driver. He did notice there were two men, the driver and a passenger. As they turned onto Main Street, they kept driving toward the business section. Porter could tell the car was a 1966 Thunderbird, a car in town he had never seen before. It was late, around 1:00 a.m. Porter thought to himself, *Who would be going down Main at this hour?* He felt uneasy.

Before turning onto 108, he decided to stay in town for a little while longer, see if the strangers stuck around, or maybe they were looking for an open gas station. He did not want to be obvious, so he stayed off Main Street and drove the dirt roads parallel to it. After half an hour he decided it was time to go home, go to bed. Tomorrow would be a busy day, he thought to himself. He drove back to Main Street and took the route he always took when leaving town.

As he entered Main Street, he saw the 1966 Thunderbird parked in front of the bank. One man was out of the car and standing near the front door of the bank, as soon as the stranger saw Porter's car, he hurriedly went back to his own vehicle, started it, and backed out. As Porter drove past, he could see in his rearview mirror the Thunderbird leaving Main Street headed the same way he was going. As he got to 108, he turned left and drove two miles then turned right and drove the four miles to where he and his parents lived. He did not see the Thunderbird again.

The next morning word spread through town. The bank had been robbed.

CHAPTER 10

The Suspects

EXCEPT FOR THE DISASTROUS 1914 fire, the most exciting moment in Glencoe history had come on a Monday morning, February 25, 1914: the attempted burglary of the Glencoe State Bank.

It could have been a perfect crime but for one small error, which resulted in a wild shoot-out. One man was killed and two others imprisoned. The action started very early. The culprits slipped into the bank unnoticed around 3:30 a.m. The robbers chopped a hole in the vault and started gathering loot. But one of the robbers accidentally knocked the receiver off an old-style phone on the vault wall. This tripped a jack in the telephone exchange at 4:00 a.m. and started a series of phone calls. The operator called Tom Brown, owner of the exchange. Brown then called Clarence McGinty, bank president. McGinty called Sheriff Emil G. Schroeder in Stillwater. Schroeder called his deputy, Joe Bradley.

At 5:00 a.m. Schroeder and McGinty were at the front door of the bank and Bradley, armed with a submachine gun, was stationed at the rear. They could see a light shining through the hole in the vault and at least one figure moving around. Schroeder yelled, "Come out with your hands up!"

Immediately bullets whistled through the bank's front window and over the officer's head. Brown shined a flashlight into the bank, and Schroeder opened fire with his repeating rifle and McGinty with his pistol. The robber immediately wormed his way through the hole in the vault and bolted out the back door.

Bradley hesitated for a moment to make sure the figure was not an officer and then shouted, "Stop or I'll shoot!" As the man continued to flee, Bradley opened fire with his submachine gun.

Soon the officers were joined by Virgil Mounts and Oke Mansfield of the highway patrol. They searched in vain for more than hour and decided the robber had escaped. But at 6:45 a.m., the patrolman found the body draped over a pile of coal in a Glencoe woman's backyard. When the woman saw the body, she screamed with such vehemence her false teeth flew out.

The dead man was identified as Ralph Davis, thirty-three, of Tulsa, who was wanted for parole violations at the time. His two accomplices, one the driver of the getaway car, were later captured and imprisoned. Officers estimate that eighty rounds of ammunition had been fired during the shoot-out. Davis's jacket was found inside the bank, bullet riddled. The bank had not been robbed again—until 1967.

The FBI sent the same two agents, Ronnie Ferguson and Steve Turner to Glencoe to investigate the bank robbery, the same two that investigated the Coyle and Oklahoma City robberies. Billy McGinty, Glencoe State Bank vice president was interviewed about logistics such as how the vault timer worked and was asked if he had seen any strangers in town. McGinty provided the information asked of him but had to say he had not seen strangers recently in his bank or around town.

The agents then began to interview the townspeople and dusted for prints in the bank. The robbers had worn gloves, leaving behind no prints; agents did find, however, that the vault had been opened using a timer device that is used to speed up a clock's time. But the agents had few clues to the crime because there were no witnesses, and there had been no hostages taken due to the hour of the robbery. The agents did not connect the Glencoe robbery to the others they were investigating; this one was committed at a different time and in a different way. The robbers had not revealed themselves, which was also different. As the agents compared notes, they decided to go to the high school to see if anyone there had noticed anything unusual during the past few weeks.

At 1:00 p.m., after the agents ate lunch at the town's café, they entered the school. The agents went to see Superintendent Howard and asked for permission to talk with the students in an assembly setting. The superintendent agreed and asked the students to meet in the gymnasium.

There, the agents identified themselves and told the students why they were there. The students had been in school all day and had learned just a few hours before that the bank had been robbed. The agents said they were looking for leads and asked the students if they had seen anything unusual in town over the course of the past month. They assured the students that they were not suspects, but the authorities would appreciate knowing anything the students may have seen or heard. Even small things one might consider to be trivial could mean a break in the case, they added, asking the students to think back carefully over the past few weeks.

Before dismissing the student body, the agents told the teenagers they would be available for the next hour. "Now, if you'd like, you can ask any questions you might have," said one of the two FBI men.

One student asked what time the robbery had occurred. "We think," said the agent, "between 1:30 a.m. and 3:00 a.m." Another asked how much had been taken, and the agents said, "That would compromise the investigation, and we will not answer the question." Another asked how the robbers had gotten into the bank, and again the agent said, "We will not answer that question, as it would compromise the investigation." The students had asked their questions, gotten few answers, and then left to go back to class.

As the students dispersed, Porter went to the lead agent, Ferguson, and told him what he'd seen: He had left town around 1:00 a.m., and as he got to the intersection of 108 and Main, he noticed a car driving slowly on 108. The car turned onto Main Street, and though it was pitch black, he could tell the car was a 1966 Thunderbird. He also told the agent he'd seen two men in the car as they'd turned onto Main; the street light had provided enough light to see the men. Porter then told Ferguson and Turner, he did not know why, but he'd had a strange feeling about the car and the men in it.

The agents asked why he had felt strange, and Porter said, "Well, it was 1:00 a.m., and nothing is open in town at that hour. I was only around because I'd had a run-in with a guy, about a girl, and was feeling a little nervous, so I decided to drive off some of my frustration. I needed to unwind before going home."

He told the agents how he had driven around town and after seeing the strangers, had decided to drive the dirt streets and not follow them directly down Main. "Then when I was ready to go home I drove down Main Street and saw the car in front of the bank," he explained.

Agent Turner asked, "Was it the same car you saw at the intersection?"

"Yes," said Porter. He then told them how he had seen a man at the bank door, but when the stranger saw his car; he went back to the Thunderbird and quickly got in.

By this time the agents were taking notes. They asked what the man at the bank door was wearing. Porter told them, "He had on a hat, not a baseball hat, one with a brim. He looked like he is in his thirties. He had on jeans and a shirt; I am not sure of the color, maybe brown."

The agents asked if Porter was good at telling how much a person weighs. "I don't know," said Porter.

"Okay," said Agent Ferguson. "How much do you think I weigh?"

Porter looked him over and said, "Maybe 165."

The agent looked at his partner and said, "He is right on. So how much did the guy you saw weigh, about, do you think?"

"I'd say he was right around your build, hard to say in the night," Porter answered.

The agent nodded and finally asked what color the car was.

"Blue with a white top, and it had spoke wheels. I told you that already, remember?"

With that he'd said everything he knew. After meeting with the agents, Porter went to his assigned class, PE. The team was already practicing, and Coach Wallace said, "You're late. Where have you been?" Porter told the coach about meeting with the two FBI agents. Wallace listened but did not say anything except to tell him to get dressed for practice.

Once Porter was dressed, he joined the team on the court. Coach Wallace split the team into "skins" versus "shirts," the subs going shirtless against the starters. The practice was grueling, and each player was sweating and panting after a short period of time. After the scrimmage, Wallace directed the players to take a rest and then huddled them to discuss the game plan against the Black Bears. As he finished, the bell rang. The players changed clothes and went to their next class.

As school was letting out, many of the students were headed to the bus line to wait for their assigned bus to take them home. Those who drove to school always parked on the south side of the school, even though it was not a designated parking lot. But it was an artificial one created by the driving students, as it was positioned so they could come and go with ease.

Keith and Rhonda left together. Rhonda was anxious to hear about the robbery and asked Keith to take her to the bank, where she could hear firsthand from her father the details of the robbery. As they drove away, Randy Clark called out to Bill and asked if he wanted to meet up in an hour and strum their guitars. John Clark left school with Pam McCubbin; Lorene Roper and David "Barbwire" Horner left together; and Dale Lyle had a new Camaro and was meeting up with the twins, Larry and Gary Murphy, who had a new Boss Mustang.

Porter left and met with Mike Crawford, Mike Phillips, Larry Shell, and Mike Wiseman at the fountain. When he arrived he found Mary Ann, Becky, Carolyn, Marsha, Linda, Gary, and Don Sosbee, who had come over to Glencoe from Wewoka to meet some girls and Bill Hodge. Gary was playing pool with Larry; the girls were in a booth watching the boys while sipping on ice cream floats. The jukebox was playing "I Can't Get No Satisfaction." As the evening went on, others came and joined the crowd. The talk was about the robbery, the game coming up against Pawnee, and what everyone would do after the game.

The FBI agents continued keeping a presence in town, but it was less visible, as they were cutting down their trips to Glencoe. The FBI office in Oklahoma City had received back a packet from the profile boys in Virginia. The information contained a profile of potential suspects who had committed the robberies in both Coyle and Oklahoma City. The profile indicated that whoever had committed the crimes likely had a desperate need for money, based on the time of day of each robbery. It also said they were risk takers, lacked self-control, since they had pistol-whipped the Coyle bank president, lacked social skills, and declared they would rely on a relative when they needed money before their next robbery. The profile predicted they would not have friends except for each other, and because of their not possessing social skills, they would need a relative who understood their quirky personalities. The report went on to say they were likely white males; this was already known information but had not been shared with the profilers. They were described as persons who would drive a flashy car to make up for their lack of social skills and to boost their own egos, and they would feel superior to others and would dress as though they had money, again to inflate their self-esteem. The packet concluded with the estimation that they would be in their mid-thirties and be unemployed.

The FBI lacked enough reliable information to issue a public bulletin describing the robbers. The profile gave them information but much of which could not be used at the time. They had to have a better description before offering the public a likely suspect description.

The FBI chief in charge of the Oklahoma City field office told the agents to run a statewide check on all 1966 Thunderbirds purchased the year before and to pay particular attention to blue Thunderbirds with white vinyl tops. Within an hour the FBI had contacted the state Motor Vehicle Registration Department to request the information they needed. When asked for the data, the clerk on the phone told the FBI agent they kept records of who purchased vehicles, the types of vehicle purchased by make and model, the ages of the purchasers, their Social Security numbers, dates of birth, and the costs of the autos. But the clerk said, "Sorry, we just don't collect information on the color of the car purchased."

The agent thanked her and asked if a rush could be initiated. "We need what information you can get us, and quick," he said.

"No problem, we will have it to you within twenty-four hours," advised the voice on the other end of the phone.

The next day Agents Ferguson and Turner received a call from the Motor Vehicle Registration Department advising them the data requested was ready to pick up. As the agents looked at the information, they were able to determine just over eleven hundred 1966 Thunderbirds had been purchased in the state of Oklahoma the year before. Just as the clerk had said they would be, they were given the names of the buyers, their ages, dates of birth, Social Security numbers, and the purchase prices. They were pleasantly surprised when the information also contained the addresses of each purchaser.

For the next three days the agents pored over the information. Nothing appeared out of the ordinary except for one purchase. The Thunderbird was bought in Tulsa, Oklahoma, and the buyer had paid cash. One of the agents found a yellow magic marker and highlighted the name, Lucille Anderson. Ms. Anderson was eighty-eight years old presently, eighty-seven at the time she'd bought the car. The FBI decided to run a credit check on her as well as a criminal background check. Within minutes they knew Ms. Anderson had no prior criminal record, and her credit check indicated she paid her bills on time, had no credit cards, spent just a few dollars per week on food, had a large savings account, and drew Social Security, which she always deposited in her checking account. Of note, she withdrew $20,000 on May 1, 1966. As the agents reviewed her information, they questioned why she would have bought a car at her age, then Agent Turner suggested they gather her medical records.

Lead Agent Ferguson placed a call to Ms. Anderson's primary care physician after his partner had obtained her Medicaid records. The agent identified himself and told the medical secretary he wanted a copy of Ms. Anderson's records. He assured the secretary the information would not be shared except on a need-to-know basis. At first the secretary was reluctant to turn over the information, but she changed her mind when the agent suggested he would get a court order and have it there within the hour. "And just so you know," he pressed, "we will bring charges against you for obstruction of justice." The secretary pulled the medical file and began making a copy for the two agents.

Later as the agents scoured the records back at their FBI office they noted Ms. Anderson had been in ill health. Her eyesight was failing, and in the record written in bold red color was, "Failing Health, Congestive Heart Disease." The FBI decided it was time to make a visit to the home of Ms. Anderson.

It was the Wednesday two days before Glencoe's game with Pawnee that the FBI agents arrived at the home of Ms. Lucille Anderson. Ms. Anderson lived in Stillwater, and the FBI knew she lived alone. The outside of her home was modest; the house was in need of a fresh coat of paint, the lawn was well maintained, large oak trees covered the front lawn with shade, and the neighborhood looked as though it had been built in the 1940s, likely after the end of World War II. Before knocking on the door, one of the agents walked to the backyard. "No garage," he said to himself.

The agents knocked on the door, no answer. They knocked again, and coming to the door was an elderly lady using a walker. The agents introduced themselves as being with the FBI. Ms. Anderson had to ask two more times for their names, and the lead agent noted she was wearing a hearing aid in addition to her black, thick-rimmed glasses.

The agents told Ms. Anderson they were investigating the Glencoe State Bank robbery and asked if she had heard about the bank being robbed. "Oh, yes," she said. "My neighbor read it in the paper and then told me. I can't read anymore; my eyes are not what they used to be."

Although up there in age, Ms. Anderson had a pretty smile and reminded the agents of their own grandmothers in years past. When Ms. Anderson asked the agents again for their names, Agent Ferguson told her I am Agent Ferguson and this is my partner Agent Turner.

"Oh what nice names," she said. "Can I get you some tea?"

"No," said Ferguson, the lead agent. "We would just like to ask you a few questions if we may." Ms. Anderson pointed to the couch, where the agents took a seat.

Ferguson asked Ms. Anderson if she drove. "No," she said, "I haven't driven in about ten years. I can't see well enough to drive." The agents then asked if she owned a car. Ms. Anderson said, "Yes, I bought one last year, but I don't drive it."

"Why did you buy a car if you're unable to drive?" Turner questioned.

"Well you see, I bought it for my son. He was down on his luck, lost his job and all, and so he asked if I could help him get a nice car. He even knew the kind he wanted." The agents exchanged a look and then asked what kind of car she had bought her son. "A Ford, I think," she said. "A real pretty one." As the conversation continued the agents asked if she remembered the color. Ms. Anderson put one finger to her to mouth and said, "A blue car, maybe even has a little white on it."

The agents completed the interview and got up to leave. On their way out the door, they stopped and thanked Ms. Anderson for talking with them, but Turner did have just another question or two to ask. "What is your son's name?"

"Gerald Allan Anderson," said Ms. Anderson. "He lives in Cushing; do you know where that is?"

"Yes," said Agent Turner, "we know. One more thing. Have any idea how much your son weighs?"

"Well I do. He calls me every Sunday, and I always ask him how he is feeling," she said. "You know, I ask if he has put on any weight. I don't get to see him much."

"That's nice," said the agent. "Did he tell you how much he weighs?"

"Oh yes, I about forgot to tell you that," the old lady said as she smiled. "He said he weighs 165, probably bigger than either of you young men . . ."

The agents again thanked her for her time and then left, wishing her a nice day.

CHAPTER 11

The Banquet

AFTER TWO WEEKS OF being punched in the arm every day by Max, the day had arrived for the Future Farmers of America banquet and the crowning of the queen, Rhonda Nichols. For two long weeks Porter had been nervous about what was to take place. The banquet was scheduled to begin at 7:00 p.m. in the high school auditorium. Plans had been made for Steve Ripley and his band to perform. Ripley attended the school and had been getting gigs across the state. The little band had a good sound and was a favorite of the Glencoe students.

The banquet would start with the awarding of medals to be pinned onto the FFA jackets of the winners, followed by the crowning, and then a sit-down meal provided by the mothers of the members of the chapter. The tables were covered with linen tablecloths, and a bouquet of flowers sat in the center of each table. Also, the mothers had supplied real silverware rather than plastic forks and knives for the place settings.

As much as Porter had tried to avoid Max the past couple of weeks it was an impossible task. The two would run into each other four or five times a day, with each meeting resulting in another "shot" to Porter's arm.

On the evening of the banquet, everyone was in a good mood. The music being played by Ripley was popular with those in attendance. Ripley had a unique sound, and he and his band played nonstop except for two five-minute breaks.

Porter had arrived thirty minutes early; this was an intentional move, as he wanted to avoid Max until it was absolutely necessary. After arriving, he made sure to stay close to several of his bigger friends.

At 8:00 p.m., the time had come: Rhonda was introduced to the crowd as the FFA Sweetheart Queen for 1967. She was in a white dress with a low cut in the back, and her blonde hair looked perfect, as she'd had it styled at the beauty parlor in Stillwater earlier in the day. Rhonda was a beautiful girl with a bright smile; no wonder Max was jealous at anyone but himself laying a hand on her.

Porter was dressed in dark-blue slacks and a white shirt with the official blue and gold FFA Tie and similarly colored jacket, which had his name engraved in gold thread. Just below the name was the word *president*. The jacket was pinned with the several medals he had earned since becoming a member in his freshman year.

The lights were dimmed, and a spotlight came up, focused on Rhonda and Porter. The two began their walk from the bleachers to the stairs leading to the stage, arm in arm. Just minutes before they began the march down the center aisle Porter looked up over his head, and to the right he saw Max sitting alone. The two spotted each other at the same time; Max had picked his spot carefully. Where he'd sat he could leave his seat without being slowed by the crowd. As Max and Porter looked at each other, Porter felt uncomfortable. He certainly had not elected Rhonda as queen just on his vote, and he knew that if he had not voted for her there would have been repercussions from Max, anyway. He was in a bind, but it was too late to do anything about it. Max did not smile when looking at Porter; it was clear he was not happy about what was about to occur.

As the couple approached the stairs, Porter extended his right hand to Rhonda while she took the five steps up onto the stage. Once the two were on stage, Porter escorted Rhonda to the center of the stage. An elementary student brought the crown to Porter, and he took it, placed it on Rhonda's hair, and swallowed deep, knowing Max was watching his every move. Finally, by the tradition, Porter kissed the new queen. He made sure the kiss was short and then quickly moved to take her arm and exit the stage to the applause of the crowd.

As the two reached the bleachers, Porter congratulated Rhonda on being elected queen and then departed into the crowd. Max had moved from his seat and was quick to get to his girlfriend. The two left, and Porter thought, *Finally this is over with*.

Ripley and his band played throughout the evening to the pleasure of those in attendance. A tarp was placed on the wooden gym floor, where dancing commenced and went on until it was time for everyone to leave.

Practices for the Pawnee game had been long and intense. Coach Wallace had developed a game plan that would attack the Bears and provide an intense defense, a full-court press. The week's scrimmages had been devoted to implementing the game plan, and Coach Wallace had been using his new video camera to record every session. Each evening before going to bed the coach would review the tape so he could make adjustments for the following day's practice.

The coach took protective measures to assure his plan would not leak out, closing the team's practices to the public. The last two days had gone well, and the players were making adjustments in stride. Each player knew their role on the court and recognized that each would play a different part in the game than they had in the game against the Pioneers.

The substitutes were drilled just as hard as the five starters, playing the part of the Bears both on offense and defense. As the game itself approached, the coach was feeling confident his team understood the new plays in the game plan, and he was equally confident they would be able to withstand any pressure applied by the Bears, giving them a good chance to beat the defending state champions.

On Thursday the day before the game, Danny Garringer returned to Glencoe. Danny had graduated two years earlier and gone to Oklahoma Baptist University, located in Shawnee, Oklahoma, on a full basketball scholarship. He was the only Panther to ever have been awarded a basketball scholarship in the history of Panther basketball. Danny knew how to play the game and knew the Panthers would be in a dogfight with the Bears.

When Danny got into town, his first stop was to the gym to watch the Panthers practice. When Coach Wallace saw him, he asked Danny to play the part of Moses Whiteagle, power forward for the Bears. Garringer stood six-foot-two, had a slender build, and could shoot the long-range ball with accuracy. The current Panthers players found Garringer hard to defend; he had a jump shot that he had perfected, was left handed, and had leaping ability. Garringer knew how to fake a shot before letting go of the ball, often baiting the opponent to make the wrong move while Garringer took aim and shot with success.

Garringer provided sound advice to the coach and the players alike. He understood the pressures of the game, the physical toll the players would experience, and knew the crowd noise would be a factor in the outcome of the game. He suggested a zone defense, except one player should play man-on-man with Whiteagle. Garringer told Wallace that Whiteagle should be pressured throughout the game and not allowed to get free, or he'd surely dominate.

After practice at the end of the evening, Larry, Keith, Bill, John, Dale, and Porter headed for on Main Street, where each had parked their car. As they exited the gym, they began to laugh about how Porter had looked nervous on stage at the banquet the previous night. Each made jokes except for Porter, who felt his ordeal with Max had finally come to an end. The conversation quickly began to center on the next day's game with Pawnee. Shell reported he had spoken with a friend who played for Yale, Pawnee's previous opponent. Shell had been told that the Pawnee players would trash talk throughout the game and it would be vital for the Panther players to keep cool heads.

Just as Shell finished, Danny Garringer and Mike Wiseman drove up. Garringer told the players he would be at the game and reminded them that the key to winning was not only to have skill but to have a game plan and to play smarter than the other team. Garringer wrapped it up by saying. "I know you guys have the tools to win the game, as long as you don't make to many turnovers."

Wiseman then chimed in, saying their pride was on the line. He reminded them of what had happened at the Pawnee Lake and said a victory would be one step they'd have to take to meet their preseason goals.

As each walked back to their car, Shell shouted out, "If we lose you know we will not be able to go back to Pawnee with our heads held high."

When the drivers started their engines and began to pull away, one following the other, each honked their horn as a show of unity.

The plan was in motion. Now the Panthers would wait for the Bears and for the game to begin.

CHAPTER 12

Rivals Meet

MUCH HAD BEEN SPECULATED by the fans of both teams in the days before the two fiery teams met. Each made their own predictions on how the game would end, and some even speculated what the final score would be. The Glencoe fans would have not imagined the Panthers could beat Pawnee, but having watched the team beat the Pioneers after being considered underdogs, their thinking had changed. We have a real chance to win this game, thought most of the Glencoe followers.

The Pawnee fans were confident; they were the defending state champions and had all of their starters back. They believed the Glencoe win against the Pioneers had been a fluke that they'd just gotten lucky. The Pawnee ace, Moses Whiteagle, had led the Bears to their first state championship in thirty years, and he was prepared to do it again. College scouts had an interest in his playing with their team after his graduation just a few months away.

Representatives from the Tulsa Hurricane, Oral Roberts University, Southwest Missouri State, and Texas Christian University were slated to be on hand to watch the game. Whiteagle knew he was a hot commodity and had every intention of showing his stuff as the scouts watched from the stands. He had scored twenty-five points against Yale in the season opener, had shot 54 percent from the floor, and had eight rebounds, similar to his average numbers from the year before.

Glencoe had never won a state championship in basketball, and it had been twenty years since they'd won the conference crown. The Panther players knew this was a different year and a different team than in the past; they had a will to win, practiced hard, were in excellent physical condition, and most importantly, they played well together as a unit. They did not consider one player more important than another and certainly did not consider themselves to be underdogs.

As the three school buses full of Panther players, cheerleaders, and pom-pom girls drove into Pawnee, they were followed by a long parade of cars full of supporters. Out the windows of the bus the players could see people lined along the street holding signs that read things like, "Looking for a miracle? It won't happen tonight." Another read, "Turn around and go back before it's too late." As the buses and parade of cars turned right at the Humpty Dumpty grocery store on Locust Street going toward the gymnasium, the number of people with signs increased. The buses pulled into the parking lot and parked. As the players began to exit the buses they heard the sounds of boos. Insults were also heard, and tempers were beginning to flare.

The players made their way into the gymnasium lobby, led by Larry Shell, who called for a quick meeting. "Listen," he said, "what we just walked through is a sample of what we're going to get on the court. Remember, stay clam, cool, and keep your focus." Shell was a senior and had experience that many of the Panthers did not have; he was also the team captain.

Wallace entered the lobby after helping the equipment boy gather their suits and shoes and told the players to go to the locker room and to stay there. The coach did not want his players exposed to any more distress, or worse yet to get injured in a scuffle.

The girls were the first to play, and the Glencoe girls' team had already demonstrated its ability and talent against the Pioneers. The Pawnee girls had finished as conference runner-ups the year before and had set a goal to be conference champs this year; they had something to prove to themselves. As the Lady Panthers took the court to warm up before the start of the game, they were confident and poised. The crowd was loud in the pregame warm-ups, and home fans outnumbered the Glencoe fan base four to one. The Bear fans had taken most of the good seats, leaving Panther supporters to sit on the upper level of the bleachers. The seating capacity of the gymnasium was fourteen hundred, every seat was filled, and people were standing in every nook and cranny they could find. The Pawnee band was there and playing the school song, "Oklahoma."

As the buzzer sounded alerting each coach they had thirty seconds to get their teams on the court to begin play, the girls circled around Wallace, who told them to be focused, play smart, and stick to the game plan. The players listened to Wallace, serious, not joking or speaking; the message spoken by Wallace was clear: "Don't screw up." Wallace finished by telling the girls their time had arrived. Practices had gone well, they had a solid game plan, and he exhorted them to play mentally tough. As the circle broke up and the starters went to the center of the court where they would jump for possession of the ball, Wallace called out, "This is it. Go get 'em!"

Lynne Sawyer was to jump for Glencoe, and on the court with her were forwards Mary Ann Shell and Becky Clark. The guards for Glencoe were Carolyn Driskel, Linda Treat, and Kay Flowers. As the referee tossed the ball in the air, Lynne went high, her fingers touched the ball as it reached its maximum height, and she tipped it to Becky. Becky grasped the basketball and tucked it in her midsection, covering it with both arms to prevent it from being knocked away by an opposing player. Having secured possession, Becky looked side to side and saw that the defenders had pulled back in a defensive position.

She then began to dribble the ball; she saw Lynne and Mary Ann move across the paint under the goal going in different directions. Becky recognized the defense, man-to-man; she would have difficulty passing to her teammates for an easy layup—Pawnee would have none of that. The Bears strategy was to allow the Lady Panthers to take the long shot while giving up nothing in the paint. The long shot was high risk and the Bears knew it. The Lady Bears were well prepared and tough; they had the players to play man-on-man.

Now, as the shot clock was ticking down, it was time to make a move. Wallace on the sideline called for play number three by holding up three fingers. Becky saw Wallace and then raised her right arm in the air with three fingers pointed toward the sky. As soon as Lynne saw the play, she broke to the basket in the paint, but as she got halfway through she stopped and reversed her movement. The Bear defender kept going, not recognizing Lynne had changed direction. Becky saw Lynne was open and bounce passed to her. Lynne easily caught the ball under the basket and made an easy shot off the glass, giving the Lady Panthers the first lead of the game. The Glencoe fans rose to their feet in unison while clapping and cheering. The Pawnee fans did not seem concerned.

The Lady Bears inbounded the ball and easily moved it across mid-court. The Panther guards were the fastest girls on the team but were not the tallest. Each Lady Bear easily stood two inches taller than her defender. So as the Lady Bear forward scanned the floor to find her teammates, she recognized that the Panthers were in a zone defense with two players under or near the basket and one assigned to the top of the key. Carolyn, the shortest of the guards, was assigned to apply pressure at the top of the arc and try to force turnovers with her speed and quick hands. She also had the ability to make quick adjustments. Linda and Kay were playing in the backcourt. Both were sophomores but had demonstrated to Coach Wallace an ability to move from side to side with ease, and each had a unique ability to anticipate where the ball was going before it was thrown. Coach Wallace had decided to use these girls after reviewing tape from the Pawnee and Yale pre-conference game.

As Carolyn was guarding the Lady Bear forward she kept an eye on where the other forwards were positioned on the court. Carolyn made a play for the ball as the girl she was defending was moving around the top of the key, dribbling, but the forward moved quickly around Carolyn, going to the basket. Both Kay and Linda saw the dodge and moved into the paint, double-teaming the forward. The Black Bear saw her two teammates open and passed off to her right, where another forward stood in the corner unguarded. This forward received the ball fluidly, took aim, and let the ball fly—game tied.

Coach Wallace called time-out. As the girls came to the sidelines they gathered around Wallace, who met them four feet from the bench, where he began to spew. "Look," he said with a whiteboard in his hand, "when you move out of position you are allowing them to have a free, uncontested shot. Stay focused and stay with the game plan," he told his team. Wallace then looked to the forwards. "Good job, but I want to see more movement; keep them chasing you." Wallace then told Linda to inbound the ball and try to get it to Kay. "Kay, I want the ball in Mary Ann's hands, got that?"

"Yes," said Kay.

"Mary Ann, you get the ball to Lynne and set up play number five."

The girls then went back to the court. The inbounds went as planned, and Kay got the ball to Mary Ann as she had been told. Mary Ann went to the top of the key; the Lady Bears spotted the change, a different point guard. Mary Ann saw Lynne to her right, who had moved to the top of the court to retrieve the ball. She began to dribble, making quick moves against her defender, and as the shot clock was quickly expiring she tossed the ball to her left into Becky's hands. Becky took a jump shot that fell short, but

Mary Ann was in position to catch the air ball and to turn and hit a short three-footer.

The Glencoe girls had retaken the lead, and when the Lady Bears attempted to toss the ball into play, the Panther guards were fierce and prevented an inbound throw. The referee blew his whistle, signaling delay of game, a turnover. The Panthers had an opportunity to increase their lead.

The game went fast but at the end of the first half, the Lady Panthers took a three-point lead into the locker room. The game had shifted lead four different times, but the Panthers remained confident. The home fans were beginning to get nervous; every time the Lady Panthers touched, the ball the Pawnee crowd would make as much noise as possible, deafening.

In the locker room Wallace told his girls, "We won the first half, but now we must win the second half. If we increase our lead I will think we are playing well . . . lose our lead and you know what I will think," he told the players. Wallace then told the girls to get tough, stop being distracted by the crowd, and to continue to play. "Play hard every second on the clock; don't quit until the buzzer ends the game," he urged his team.

Still, Wallace was nervous as the girls left the locker room to take a few shots before the game resumed. He rolled his sleeves up and had a towel that he kept on his shoulder.

As the second half began Becky started with a designed play drawn up at halftime. She raised two fingers in the air and slapped the ball; Mary Ann and Lynne knew the play, the same play they had started the game with, except Mary Ann would break to the goal, stop, and catch the pass from Becky, where she would have a clean shot. But as Mary Ann made her break to the paint she was elbowed in the stomach, falling to the ground. The referee called time-out.

Wallace came on the court to ask his player if she could continue. He was not satisfied that she could, and with assistance, he got her off the court, where others took her to the locker room. Wallace then called for Marilyn Childers to enter the game. Meanwhile he argued with the referees that the elbow had been thrown intentionally and the player should be thrown out of the game. As the coach continued to make his point, the Pawnee crowd started booing him and yelling for him to get off the court.

The referee was paying little attention, and he turned away when Wallace moved in front of him and put his finger in his chest. The referee immediately made a *T* with his two hands, signaling a technical foul and telling Wallace if he said one more thing he would be ejected from the game. Retreating to the bench, Wallace took his tie off and threw it at his feet, all the while the crowd calling for his ejection.

The coach reached up with one hand and brushed his hair back while mumbling to himself under his breath. The head referee approached Wallace and told him Glencoe would get one free shot for the foul to Mary Ann, and then the ball would be handed over to the Lady Bears to shoot two free throws. Following the free throws the ball would stay with the Bears to inbound. Wallace told Marilyn to take the one free throw; when a player who was fouled was injured and could not attempt the free throw, the rules allowed the coach to pick any player of his choosing to shoot for the injured player.

Marilyn stepped to the free throw line. She had been shooting well in practices and during the pre-game warm-ups. She bounced the ball two times, focused on the goal, and let the shot go. She scored. The referee took the ball and went to the other end of the court, where the Bears had two free throws to shoot. As the player stepped to the line she took her first shot, a miss. She was handed the ball again, but before shooting, the Lady Bear forwards stepped up to her said a few words. The girl went back to the line, shot, and made a clean hit. The referee then took the ball and gave it to the Lady Bears to inbound.

The Bears in bound and scored another quick two points. After a couple more exchanges that went well for the Bears, the Panthers lost the lead, trailing by three. But Glencoe took possession of the ball and scored easily, and as the Bears in bound the ball, Carolyn's quick hands stole it. She dribbled to half court and passed off to Becky, who shot and made, and the Panthers again led by one. The Black Bear ladies easily scored on the next trip. As the Panthers again took possession, Becky began to dribble toward the basket, but she was cut off; she passed off to Lynne, who quickly tossed the ball to Marilyn. With the shot clock running down, Becky caught Marilyn's pass and drove to the basket. She leaped into the air and tossed the ball backward over her head, where Marilyn stood at the free throw line. Marilyn caught it and had a natural screen with Becky in front of her; she took the shot and scored. The Panthers led once again.

It was tight until the fourth quarter began, when the Lady Panthers got back in their groove; the Bears seemed to run out of gas and were not the same team that had started the game. As the fourth quarter ticked away, the Lady Panthers' shooting percentage increased to a sizzling 56 percent, while the Lady Bears dropped to hitting just one in three shots. The Bears' legs looked tired, and their jump shots were short. Their ability to rebound had decreased, while the Panthers seemed to be gaining strength.

When the game ended, the Panthers celebrated a fourteen-point win, a solid victory. As the girls entered the locker room, they asked how Mary Ann was feeling and were told her parents had taken her home, she was not there. Mary Ann learned of the win later that night when Lynne called her with the good news.

Coach Wallace entered the boys' locker room, where he had instructed them to stay while the girls had played. "The girls won," he told the boys. "It wasn't easy, but they did it." Wallace then told them the crowd was angry and they would be a factor in their game. "Their fans came to see a victory, and they will make noise like you have never heard before." Before they left the locker room Wallace asked his team if anyone had anything to say before hitting the court.

"I do," said Shell.

"Go for it," said Wallace.

The team captain said, "We have a chance to show everyone who believes in us, everyone who has ever worn the blue and gold that we have learned from them. Let's play for them."

Wallace then told the players to go out with their heads held high. "I want every player to be holding the hand of another as we enter the court," he explained. "Let's show them we are one team, a united one. Now let's hit the court!"

As the players stepped onto the court they were greeted with cheers from the Glencoe fans and jeers from the opposing team's crowd. Someone was heard yelling, "Billy boy, this is not going to be your night." The heckler was referring to Bill Hodge, center for the Panthers.

Someone else called out, "Go home while you still can." The players heard the crowd and the insults but continued to focus on their pre-game warm-ups. The Black Bears were on the opposite end of the court, their star, Moses Whiteagle, stood at half court and glared at the Panthers. Whiteagle knew both Hodge brothers from reputation and from the night at the lake where Keith had confronted him. As he continued to stand at center court, glaring, he would smirk and point to a Panther player whenever he missed a shot or a layup. Soon two of his teammates joined him with the mild taunts.

The Hodge brothers, Shell, Porter, Lyle, Clark, and Mitchell continued on as if they were the only ones on the court. With thirty seconds remaining before tip-off, Wallace called his players to the sideline. They circled around Wallace, making the coach seem small. He looked up to see into their eyes as he gave his final instruction: "Play hard and play smart." The players then took their positions on the court.

Mike Wiseman entered the circle where the ball would be tossed in the air; his competition was Moses Whiteagle. Wiseman had the height advantage, but barely. Whiteagle had the experience, being a senior, and had been given credit for leading his Bears to last year's state championship game and ultimately winning it. As the ball was tossed in the air, Wiseman jumped first, getting a good lead.

Whiteagle's jump sent him slightly sideways, bumping Wiseman. "Redo!" yelled the referee.

The crowd was quiet as the players re-jumped. This time as the ball was tossed in the air Whiteagle did not jump; he moved out of the circle to add to the number of Bears who could catch the center's tip as it was sent to the standing players waiting to catch the ball. The plan worked; Whiteagle was able to crowd out one of the Panthers as the ball was heading his direction.

As the Bears took control in the opening seconds of the game, they spread the court. Wallace immediately figured out that the opponent was going for a slow tempo, something he had not anticipated. As he watched from the sideline, he smiled and thought to himself, *They have watched film on us and know we can run with them all day; smart move on their part.* But Wallace had prepared for the game, as well, based on talking with and getting film from the Yale coach.

Whiteagle moved the ball downcourt with the Panthers applying intense pressure by putting on a full-court press. The Bears were used to the pressure as they had faced Newkirk the year before in the state championship game, who had also used the press. Whiteagle eyed the court, moving to the top of the arc and looking to the other four players, who were moving in and out of the paint, going to the corners, and then moving again to open areas on the court. Shell began to apply the man-on-man defense against Whiteagle, as suggested by Garringer.

Whiteagle began to make a move, dribbling first behind his back and then through his legs. As the ball exited his legs, his left hand secured it, but he quickly shifted it to his right. While dribbling, one of the remaining players came to the arc and set a screen on Shell; Whiteagle then pick-and-rolled, going into the paint and toward the bucket. The other Panthers, playing a zone defense, quickly moved in on him to block his path. Whiteagle was within five feet of the basket when he took off into the air. Bill saw the move and quickly positioned himself in front of Whiteagle, froze like a statue, and Whiteagle plowed into him, knocking him to the floor. The referee was on top of the action and blew his whistle. "Charge!" he called. The ball was turned over to Glencoe for their first possession of the game.

Gary Mitchell for the Panthers tossed the ball to Shell, who deliberately took his time bringing the ball down the court, a strategy put in place as part of Wallace's game plan to take the Bears out of their tempo. As Shell crossed center court he raised one finger in the air and shouted, "One!"

Wiseman, the tallest player on the Panther squad, went to the center line and then cut toward the basket. The Bears did not bite; the Bear guarding Wiseman stayed on his trail while the remaining four players stuck with their assignments. Seeing the play would not work, Shell stuck a closed fist in the air. Bill immediately waited for the ball to be thrown to him, as the new play called for. Shell was able to get him the ball, and then Bill tossed the ball in the air toward the goal as if taking a shot—although the play was designed for Wiseman to come flying in, catch the ball in midair, and then make a clean dunk. It worked, and Glencoe led by two points.

Following the score, Wallace called a time-out. "Why is he calling time?" asked Childers to Driskel, who was sitting next to him. "We are up by two and are playing good on the defensive end of the court."

Driskel responded with, "Wallace must have seen something and wants to give the players a heads-up."

The players gathered around their coach, who told them, "Now go into a full zone defense; we want to keep them off balance."

After the time-out, Lucas Dobson took charge of the ball for the Bears and took the ball downcourt, again being contested all the way by a press. The Panthers settled into a zone with two players at the top of the key, two below the basket, and one playing in between. Whiteagle saw the zone defense and felt insulted. *These guys think they can play as well as us, so they have shifted defenses?* thought Whiteagle.

Dobson handed off to Whiteagle, who thought he could show his quickness, strength, and ball handling abilities to the scouts in the stands with a quick move to the basket, followed by a jump-stop at the top of the key and a shot. The ball bounced off the back of the glass and then into the cylinder. Game tied.

As the game continued, both teams were playing their best basketball of the early season, both shooting well and equal in rebounds. The Panthers had a slight edge in second-shot chances. At the second quarter, the two teams were tied, and both remained strong physically, no exhaustion on the part of either team. Between quarters, the Bears decided to spread the court, pass often, and only shoot when the shot was available. To start the second quarter, Dobson again brought the ball downcourt to the offensive end of the floor. As he crossed the line, he stopped to take a long jump shot. The shot missed and was recovered by the Panthers.

The Pawnee coach called time, his first of the game. As the players went to the sidelines he pulled Dobson to him by his collar. "Didn't I say to be patient, not shoot until there was an opening?"

"Yes sir," said Dobson.

"Then why didn't you? Go sit down and think about it for a while," said the Bears coach. He then called for Adam Hampton to enter the game. Hampton entered the game with experience and talent. He had played with Whiteagle for several years and knew the moves Whiteagle would make. After having gotten in the game Hampton took a shot that was all air, within the next two minutes he was called for a foul, missed a second shot and had the ball stolen from him while casually dribbling down court. Shortly afterwards Dobson was back in the game. While sitting on the bench being embarrassed he had watched the panthers pull off play after play and he found what he thought was a weak spot in the Panther defense. Dobson quickly took control of the ball and along with Whiteagle was on the verge of taking control of the game. As Whiteagle brought the ball down court he saw Dobson alone in the corner, as he dribbled toward the goal he quickly kicked the ball to Dobson who with confidence took the shot and scored.

Glencoe now had possession, and the Bears had started applying more defensive pressure than at any point in the game. As Mitchell for the Panthers looked to inbound, Lyle made a break to the other end of the court. Mitchell saw Lyle make his move and threw long; Lyle let the ball hit the floor one time before taking hold of the ball, taking a dribble amidst three steps, and then dunking the ball. The Glencoe fans exploded with applause and whoops and hollers. The Pawnee fans grumbled their dissatisfaction.

Before the Bears put the ball in play, they quickly huddled at mid-court, except for Whiteagle, who was angry at his teammate for allowing Lyle to break from the pack and get an easy dunk. Whiteagle looked at his teammates and said, "What is wrong with you? Are you here to play or to let them score points? If you do that again I will kick your butt." The other players were offended. Yes they had come to play and to win, but Whiteagle was making it personal with his own teammates. Dobson took offense at the remark and warned Whiteagle they were to play as a team and for Whiteagle to stop intimidating his own team members.

The Pawnee players then set up for the inbound pass. The player tossing in the ball attempted to lob the ball high to Whiteagle, but Wiseman was there and took it from his hands, just as he thought he had it secured. Wiseman and his teammates moved into offensive position, where Wiseman threw high into the hands of Bill, who had an easy dunk.

Whiteagle was furious. *I will take control of the game,* he said to himself. *Looks like I am the only one who can.* Glencoe had a growing lead, while the Bears were becoming frustrated. Dobson tried to bring back the bears but Whiteagle was too busy trying to impress the college scouts to pass off to his own team members.

At halftime the Panthers led by six. In their locker room, Wallace was sweating, and he had a nervous laugh. He told his team it would be important to keep the pressure on. "If we did not have a halftime and kept playing, we would have won the game. They are rattled," he said. "But now they can regroup, settle in, and they will come out like a lion. Be ready for them."

In the Bear locker room, the coach told his players to settle down. "We are still in this game, and we can win it," he encouraged.

Whiteagle then began to spew his own words, telling the coach and his teammates they had to do better and they had been playing like a bunch of babies. The other players took issue with Whiteagle, telling him they were a team of five, not one. "Like you would want it," said Dobson.

Glencoe came out with a full-court press but switched back to the partial zone defense, with one player tailing Whiteagle wherever he went. As the Bears set up on the offensive end of the court, the Panthers looked fresh. They had done their job so far.

Whiteagle dribbled for a while, not passing off to any of his teammates. He finally saw an opening and sped through the hole, making a layup. The Panthers then took possession and easily moved down court. Shell slapped the ball two times, signaling for all players to move. Lyle crossed into the paint, turning to the free throw line, where Shell tossed the ball to him. Lyle spun around and took a short, ten-foot jump shot. Glencoe had just gotten back the two points they'd given up to the Bears. The game continued, with each team countering the other's scoring abilities. At the end of the third quarter, Glencoe had held onto its six-point lead.

Between the third and fourth quarters the Pawnee band had began to play loud and often, making an attempt to rally the spirits of their beloved Bears by playing the school song, "Oklahoma." Whiteagle continued to handle the ball most of the fourth quarter, passing seldom to his teammates, though throughout the first three quarters he had been held to eight points, one assist, and two rebounds, way below his average from a year ago and in the first game of this season. He was aware he was not making an impression with the scouts on hand and felt mounting frustration as the clock continued to tick away, along with his hopes of a future basketball career.

With seven minutes remaining in the game, the Bears became aggressive by pushing, elbowing, and tripping the Panther players at times when the referees were not positions to see the rough play. With five minutes left the Bears had inched closer, tightening the score to a four-point deficit. On one play, a Panther passed the ball to Bill, who went up for what would be an easy lay-up—except for the shot he took to his jaw. Bill went to the floor hard, banging his head. The referee saw the assault and ejected the offending player. Wallace got on the court, screaming at the official even though the correct call had been made.

Bill had temporarily lost consciousness. Though he awakened quickly, he was unable to gather his senses and could not answer basic questions asked of him, such as, Where are you? What is your name? And can you stand? Minutes later, after Bill had recovered a bit and was helped off the court, Wallace called for Porter to enter the game as Bill's replacement, telling him to go to the free throw line and shoot the two free throws that had been awarded.

Porter stepped to the line. The Bear fans began to make deafening noise, stomping their feet on the wooden bleachers and shouting insults. Porter took a deep breath and slowly exhaled while releasing the ball; his first shot was good. The referee bounced the ball back to him. Porter once again took the ball, eyed the basket, and controlled his breathing. The second shot was good as well, and now the clock showed two minutes of game left. With time running out the Panthers still had a lead of six points.

Dobson came down the court and hit all net from thirty feet out. The Panthers came back downcourt but missed their shots the next two possessions, while the Bears found success on one of the two trips. The game was in reach for the Bears, down by two, with just thirty seconds left they hit another goal: game tied. The Panthers' next trip came up empty, their shooting touch falling cold at just the wrong time. With ten seconds left, the Bears had the ball and could win the game with a field goal or by getting fouled and making a free throw.

Whiteagle crossed center court holding onto the ball until he saw the opening he had waited all night for. As he made a move to the bucket, he went flying, releasing the ball in the air. As the ball was still going upward, Porter jumped and swatted it with his left hand, sending the ball back downcourt and hoping the clock would run out and the teams would go into overtime.

As the ball went flying, two Panthers and one Bear chased it, but on the way the Black Bear player collided with a Panther. Lyle was the Panther free to get to the ball before it went out of bounds. He caught it on its second bounce and drove to the basket; he had three seconds. He was able to accelerate, go high, and put through an easy layup off the glass. As the ball fell to the floor after going through the net, the buzzer sounded, ending the game. Glencoe had won by two last-second points.

"Get off the court!" shouted Wallace to his team. Before the players could exit the gym to get on board their bus, they'd have to move through a mob atmosphere. The insults continued the same as they had when the team had first arrived to play the game. As the Panthers left the court, they saw Whiteagle verbally attacking his fellow players, challenging them to a fistfight.

Once on the bus each player found a seat for the trip back to Glencoe. The girls and boys were not restricted to separate buses, and the two teams' players found seats next to each other. When the buses exited town on Highway 64, the bus drivers found a long stream of cars lined up behind them with their lights on and honking in celebration. As they arrived back at the school, Superintendent Howard unlocked the entrance door and invited everyone into the gym.

Superintendent Howard announced he had been hoping for a win and had made preparations for balloons to be hung from the rafters, the concession stand to be in operation, and a tarp to be put on the wooden gym floor for dancing. Howard said he wanted the players and fans to have a place to celebrate in a friendly atmosphere. One of the players located a stereo and put on rock and roll. Everyone celebrated the big wins for the next three hours. Following the party, everyone left in a festive mood to return to their homes.

CHAPTER 13

The Raid

THE FBI HAD ALERTED the Cushing Police Department of their plan to raid the home of Gerald Allan Anderson in the late afternoon of the coming Sunday. After the plan was revealed, the chief was requested to provide manpower with the setting up of a roadblock covering a three-block area, to stop all incoming and outgoing traffic. At 8:00 p.m. on Sunday night the two agents and five SWAT team members from the FBI encircled the Anderson home, each equipped with bulletproof vests, 9-millimeter revolvers, walkie-talkies, and flashlights. The squad van also contained a door rammer made of steel in the event it would be needed to break down the front door.

One FBI agent approached the front porch wearing a pizza delivery boy uniform. In the front of the house the agent parked a beat-up two-door Ford Falcon equipped with a neon sign on the roof that read "Pizza Delivery." When the agent got to the door he was able to see a dim light with no shade in the entryway of the house. A 1964 Mercury Comet, beige in color, was in the driveway, but no Thunderbird.

The agent knocked on the door. No answer. Again he knocked while shouting, "Pizza Delivery." The agent saw the doorknob begin to turn, and the curtain looking over the porch was being pulled back. When the door opened a young lady in her mid-twenties appeared, holding a baby girl of maybe six months. The baby was wearing only a diaper, and from the odor, the diaper was soiled. The child had crusted milk around her mouth and a red rash that appeared to be from insect bites. The mother of the child wore tight blue jeans and a tank top and had her hair in a ponytail.

As she opened the door, the agent pressed the electronic clicker in his hand two times. The clicker did not make any noise but sent a radio transmission to the SWAT team by beaming a red, flashing light. Each member of the team carried one of these signaling devices for tactical purposes. When the swat team received the signal, they quickly converged on the house; two went to the front door, where the lead agent was, and two went to the back door in case anyone in the house made an attempt to escape. The other members of the team maintained their positions.

The young lady with the baby immediately said she had not ordered pizza; the delivery driver must have made a mistake and gone to the wrong house. The agent then identified himself and asked if anyone else was in the home. "No" she said, "I am the only one here."

The agent said he had a search warrant and asked her to step aside, which she did, then the agent and two SWAT team members entered the home. The agents went from room to room looking in drawers, closets, and under the bed and anywhere they thought a person could be hiding or where they might have hidden items of special value.

While the others searched the house, one of the agents took the young mother and her child to the side, where she was asked her name. "I am Debbie Metzger," she said. "Why are you here?"

"We have reason to believe this house has been used by two men we are looking for."

"For what?" Debbie said angrily.

"Bank robbery and assault and battery," said the agent. The agent then told her she would be charged with harboring fugitives from justice and obstruction of justice, but they could make a recommendation to the prosecutor's office to reduce her charges if she cooperated and did not withhold information or evidence.

The agent began a more formal, serious interview. "Let's start from the beginning. What is your name?"

"Debbie Metzger."

"Do you own this house?"

"No, I rent it."

"Who lives with you?" the agent asked.

The young woman said, "I live alone with my baby."

The agent's face became still more serious. "I want to repeat that we have reason to believe you are involved in harboring fugitives and may be charged with being an accessory to more than one crime. Do you understand?"

"Yes," Debbie said with a nod.

"Then try again; do you have anyone living with you and your child?"

"Yes," the woman admitted.

The agent nodded and then said, "Good. Now how many people?"

"Two men."

"Their names?"

"Gerald Anderson and Leroy Johnson."

"Good, now where are they?"

Debbie shook her head. "I don't know, they said they were leaving for a little while and would be back."

"When did they leave?"

"About an hour before you came knocking."

"Do you think they are in town?" the agent asked.

"Sometimes they will go to the Okie Breeze, a local bar, to drink and hang out."

With that the agent then radioed the Cushing chief of police and advised him to contact the county child protective services office. He told them, "We have a six-month baby who is filthy, and the child's mother is being arrested and will be detained."

"Yes sir," said the chief.

While the agents continued to comb the house looking for anything that could help them with their investigation, Leroy Johnson and Gerald Anderson were at the local pub drinking beer and flirting with the bar hostess. Johnson ran out of cigarettes and asked a patron, Angie Freeney, to take him to buy a pack of smokes. Gerald was too wasted to drive and was aware it would be a major problem if he was pulled over for DUI.

Freeney and Johnson took off in her 1962 Malibu. They drove by the street that would have taken Johnson home, and Johnson saw the road was blocked off, with a police car parked in the middle of the street to prevent any cars from entering. Johnson told Freeney to drive around the block; there he saw the street was again blocked off by one of Cushing's finest police officers. "Go back to the bar, and step on it," said Johnson.

Freeney looked over at her passenger and saw him beginning to sweat; he was fidgety and looked nervous. "What's wrong with you?" she asked. "I thought you wanted some smokes, and then I thought, well, you know . . ."

"No I don't know," said Johnson. "Just shut up and drive."

When they got back to the bar Johnson went to Anderson and told him what he had just seen. "The road leading back to the house is blocked off with cops. Something is wrong; we need to go now."

The men went out the back door of the Okie Breeze to where they had parked, got in the Thunderbird, and sat for a moment. "We didn't tell Debbie where we were going, did we?" asked Anderson.

"Hell no," said Johnson. "We will have to leave town by going out on the back streets. Get on the country back roads and get us out of the state."

The FBI continued to search the house and found men's clothing, cigarette butts of different brands, beer and whiskey in the kitchen cabinets, and a map of the state of Oklahoma showing Coyle, Oklahoma City, and Glencoe highlighted in yellow. Other communities—Perkins, Thomas, Shawnee, and Yukon—were highlighted in blue. As the agents looked at the map, they believed they had found some evidence of where the next targets were going to be. The lead agent radioed the chief of police and told him, "Take as many men as you can muster to the Okie Breeze. We think that is where they are right now. Have your dispatcher get a hold of child protective services again; they have not gotten here yet, and I don't want to tie up manpower any longer watching over this baby."

The Cushing Police Department sent four cars to converge on the bar. Two parked in the front and two in the back. The chief of police and another officer approached the front door to the bar. They pulled their revolvers in case the criminals weren't going to surrender without a fight. The officers in the back exited their car and took a defensive position behind it and the waste disposal container. Two FBI agents also arrived and parked on the street out front.

As the officers in front entered through the door, the patrons stopped what they were doing and just stared at the cops. The barmaid set down a bottle of rum on the counter; a man and a woman sitting at the end of the bar stopped talking and turned to look at the officers; four people at a round table who had their backs to the door stopped when they saw the others staring and put down their drinks. The two officers looked into the eyes of each person there, one by one, and the chief said, "I'm looking for two men, mid-thirties, five-foot-ten or so, slender builds. I was told they were here. Anybody seen them?"

The bartender said there had been two men there just a short time ago. "But they left a bit ago, and in a hurry," she added.

"When?" asked the chief.

"Fifteen minutes or so," she said. About that time Angie Freeney entered the bar after having gone to the bathroom. The barmaid pointed to Angie and said, "She took one of them somewhere; she can tell you more about that."

The chief went to Angie and asked, "Have you seen Gerald Anderson and Leroy Johnson?"

"I know the one you call Johnson; he needed a pack of cigarettes, and I took him to buy a pack. Strange dude," she said.

"Why do you say that?" asked the chief.

"As I was driving him to the honk and holler to get his cigs, we passed by 10th and Hudson Streets, and suddenly he freaked."

"How do you mean, freaked?" asked the chief

"He got nervous, started sweating, told me to circle the block, and then he told me to take him back to the bar. When we got here he ignored me, like I wasn't even around."

"What happened then?" ask the officer.

"He went to this other guy . . . maybe his name is Gerald or Jerry, something like that. I didn't quite catch it. They talked for a few seconds, and wham bam thank ya ma'am they were gone."

"Do you know what kind of car they were in?"

"No, they went out the back, and I haven't seen them since. Good riddance, I say."

The witness could give them no more help. The officers left the bar, went to the FBI agents parked in the street, and told them what they had just learned. "Okay," said the agent. "They are on to us, so now they're gone. Chief, set up roadblocks on the streets that lead out of town. Call the Oklahoma Highway Patrol and tell them to be on the lookout for the blue 1966 Thunderbird. Think you can get that done in the next couple of minutes?"

"Sure," said the chief, and then he got on his car radio and put out the word to his officers before calling the highway patrol regional office in Pawnee to advise of the need for assistance.

CHAPTER 14

Uncle Sam Calls

T HE LOCAL SWIMMING HOLE, Yost Lake, had closed for the season, as fall had arrived and the nights were becoming cooler and cooler. The daytime temperatures were still in the seventies, while nighttime temperatures were dipping into the mid-forties. Yost Lake was a private lake and was surrounded by one-story, wooden cabins owned by people from out of town who went to the lake on weekends or holidays or spent a few days there while taking vacation. The lake area was small, approximately fifty acres. On the grounds was a small, nine-hole golf course, a tennis court, an outdoor basketball court, a pavilion for barbequing or dancing, and just off the pavilion was a waterslide.

On the Saturday morning following the game against Pawnee, the players, cheerleaders, pom-pom girls, and others looking for something to do on a Saturday night all seemed to be calling each other up, looking for plans. Porter called Mike Crawford and Jimmy Arias to see if they wanted to get everybody together. "Let's go to Yost," said Porter as he talked to Jimmy.

"Sounds good, but it's closed," Jimmy responded.

"Never stopped us before," said Porter. "You call the Hodge brothers, Shell, and his sister Mary Ann and ask them to spread the word."

"Sure," said Jimmy. "I'm on it."

After talking to Mike Crawford and Mike Phillips, Porter called Randy and Wiseman and told them of the plan to meet at Yost that evening. "Let's meet on Main," said Porter. "From there we can head out together."

When evening arrived, everyone who had a car showed up on Main. Those who didn't hitched a ride; no one wanted to miss the party of the year. As the cars rolled down Main, each parked by backing up into the spaces in front of the bank and the post office. The last to arrive was Keith, who had gone to pick up his steady, Rhonda.

"How are we going to get through the gate leading into the lake? It's padlocked," stated Marty Matlock.

"I brought bolt cutters," said Porter. "You get with Randy and make a run out there, cut the lock, and head back here when you're finished."

Marty and Randy jumped in Marty's 1963 Mustang and took off. The fifty or so teenagers remained on Main Street, turned their radios to KOMA, and started a street dance. Just as the dancing got underway, Steve Ripley drove up. "Hey, I got the word about the party tonight. I've been working at the Perry Sale Barn today and thought you might want a little live music," he said, grinning.

"Sure!" said Porter. "Do you have your guitar?"

"Yep," said Ripley. "Brought the Gibson." As the radios continued to blare, Ripley began to play along with his guitar.

After an hour Marty and Randy drove back into town, honking and flashing their car lights as they approached. Marty rolled down the window to his Mustang and yelled, "Lets go, party time!"

As the cars began to fill up with drivers and passengers, each headed to the lake and when arriving found the gate unlocked. The cars slowly drove in and parked near the pavilion. Randy and Marty had made sure no one was staying at the lake in a cabin for the weekend; no one was there, so the lake belonged to them for the evening.

Ripley went to the pavilion and set up his guitar, plugging in to an electric amplifier he had brought along for the occasion. He opened with "Mama Told Me Not to Come," and while he rocked out, the dancing began. On the pavilion near the water, Rhonda was dancing with Keith. Kay was with Luke, Linda Treat with Charles Robinson, John was with Pam, Donna was with Kelly, and Wesley Fritchman was with Kathy Turner. Over in the corner Vickie Beverage was trying to talk Mike Crawford into getting on the dance floor; Mike was stalling as long as he could until Vickie took his hand and pulled him to center stage. Mary Ann Shell had brought a friend, whom she introduced around the pavilion as Jon Brock. Also there was Becky with a guy from Perkins named Phil Hughes, a friend of Porter's.

While the dancing was going on, Porter and Marty went to the water, dipped their toes in to check the temperature, and declared it was warm enough to swim in. "It may be a little cold," said Porter, "but you will get used to it quick."

After Mike escaped the dance floor, he came over to Porter and said, "I have something to say." Mike was serious as he began telling Porter about when he graduates in May he was going to sign up with Uncle Sam.

"What?" said Porter. "Have you thought about this?"

"Yes," said Mike, serious. "I have talked to an Army recruiter, and he said they have a new program called the Buddy System. If someone goes in with me we can be assured we will go through boot camp together."

"Of course they would do something like that; they need all the volunteers they can get with that Southeast Asia thing," said Porter. "So, is somebody else gonna join with you?"

"Yeah, Wesley Fritchman and Orville Payne. Anyway, I wanted you to know. And there is something else."

"Okay. What is it?" asked Porter.

"We already signed the papers; we will be sent to boot camp in June, going to Fort Sill and then Fort Bragg, North Carolina. I want to do some parachuting and let Uncle Sam pay for it."

Suddenly Porter felt the party, which had been so much fun, had been turned into a "funeral".

As 11:00 p.m. turned to midnight, many of the partygoers had left or were leaving, as they had curfews at home. Others stayed, like Mike, Wesley, Orville, Eddie, and Jimmy Arias. The five popped open a Coors apiece and began to chug the beers. Porter tried to tell them they had no idea what was about to happen. "Do you guys know where you're going?" he asked.

"Sure we do," said Wesley. "We're going to boot camp and then to Fort Bragg to jump out of airplanes."

"You might do some jumping, all right," said Porter. "When you're getting shot at over in Nam. Remember John Marlow? Less than three weeks, that's all it took."

"Enough," said Mike, "we're here for some fun, so drop the subject. Besides, the night before we leave for boot camp I can see a party in the future, a real blast."

When the five had finished the twelve-pack they jumped in their cars and drove back to Glencoe, where they went to Main and parked to hang out for a little while longer. As they talked about the party—and in particular, Keith having danced himself off the pavilion into the lake—the conversation soon got back to Vietnam. "I admire you guys, but why don't you go to college or at least join the Guard instead of the regular Army?" Porter asked.

"We are not interested in going to college, graduating, and then sitting behind a desk for the next forty years. And as far as the Guard, that's for weekend warriors. Since we decided already we might as well go into the big leagues, get a little sightseeing in, and receive training that we can use when we get out," said Orville.

"You know we have had some good times and there will be plenty more to come," said Mike. "Remember our deal in baseball? You on the mound and me on third, you get the outs and we will get the runs."

"Yeah," said Porter, reminiscing.

"I will make you another deal," said Mike. "We go protect our freedom by keeping the Commies from taking over Asia and spreading to other countries, and you go to college and make sure we have jobs when we get back."

"Deal," said Porter, "but only if we have one heck of a going-away party before you leave."

"You got it," said Mike.

CHAPTER 15

Empty-handed

THE AGENTS RETURNED TO their offices in Oklahoma City empty-handed; they had fully expected to have the two fugitives in custody before arriving back. "Now that we know the names of both thugs, let's run a background check on Johnson and see if there is anything new on Anderson," said the FBI chief. "Send the fingerprints you gathered at the house to the lab boys. Maybe they can give us a match to other crimes."

The Oklahoma Highway Patrol had broadcast to all of its troopers to be on the lookout for a blue '66 Thunderbird with two male passengers in their mid-thirties. The passengers were described as likely armed and dangerous. As soon as the troopers received the urgent message, their patrolling of the state's two-lane highways and interstates intensified. Now they were on the watch for the dangerous suspects, not just speeders.

One week following the FBI lab's receiving the fingerprints of both Anderson and Johnson; they were able to say with certainty that the prints matched an individual who was believed to be involved in a bank robbery that had occurred two years earlier in Durango, Colorado. The report further indicated a match to a bank robbery in Springer, New Mexico, one year ago. The suspects became more wanted than ever when the FBI agents saw that the Durango robbery had gone bad, and a bank employee had been killed when pistol-whipped by one of the robbers.

The agents in Oklahoma City knew the two men had experience in bank robbery, and now the search had to be expanded to include states across the Oklahoma border. The report from the profilers a few weeks ago was right on when it said the criminals would be dangerous when feeling they had been backed into a corner.

The agents placed calls to officials in New Mexico and Colorado and learned that each state had had three bank robberies, including the ones the FBI already knew about. Authorities in each state told the agents the robberies all had a similar signature; they believed each robbery had been committed by the same two men. The FBI concluded that Anderson and Johnson's confidence had grown; they were becoming more brazen with each robbery.

The FBI office and agents in Oklahoma City were confident Anderson and Johnson would make a break for another state, likely one bordering Oklahoma. They ruled out New Mexico and Colorado since the robbers were unlikely to go where they'd already been and were wanted. More likely would be Missouri, Arkansas, or Texas, the first two because of the mountainous areas in those states, and Texas because of its dense population centers. They staffed the case with their superiors and got ready to continue the manhunt.

CHAPTER 16

Running Alone

A T BASKETBALL PRACTICE ON the Monday following the victory over Pawnee, Coach Wallace held up the *Stillwater NewsPress* sports page. The headline read, "Panthers on a Roll." The article went on to say the team was playing at a higher level than in past years, that they played with poise, had a strong bench, and if they continued on the same victorious path, it would be a shoot-out with Morrison, perennial conference power. "The Panthers and Tigers will be in a fight that rivals the gunfight at the OK Corral, but without the guns, thank God."

The players sat and listened as Coach Wallace read the article with pride, all of them confident they would stay on the unbeaten path. When Wallace finished with the column he told the players, "Our next game is in conference play; Kaw City will be waiting for you." He told his team Kaw City was 1–1 in pre-season play, having beaten Apache and losing to Big Cedar. Wallace had watched film of both their games and was impressed with the physical conditioning of the Kaw City players. He said, "We must be able to stop them, and the only way to do that is to have better conditioning than they do." He then said, "Never take your opponent lightly; if we underestimate them based on their win–loss record we will be making a big mistake. They are better than their record indicates. They had opportunities to win but they squandered too many plays, too many turnovers. You can bet Coach Miller will have that corrected by the time we meet them."

Following his speech, Wallace instructed the players to run twenty laps around the court, followed by stop-and-go sprints from one end of the court to the other. During the one-hour practice, Wallace made sure no one touched a basketball.

The next day the players discussed how difficult practice had been the day before and how tough it was going to get until their bodies adjusted to the new workout schedule. Porter announced he was going to begin running a few miles a day to help with his overall conditioning. He did not know at the time that running alone could be dangerous to his health.

CHAPTER 17

The Great Escape

As the FBI and Oklahoma Highway Patrol continued their manhunt, the fugitives decided to stay in Oklahoma. "They expect us to leave," said Anderson, "but we still have business here."

"What are you talking about?" asked Johnson.

"There is a kid out there who got a look at our car. The kid saw me when I was standing at the bank door; he can identify me. Get rid of him and there is no witness," said Anderson. Both Anderson and Johnson were unaware Porter had already talked to the FBI and told them everything he had seen.

The robbers drove twenty miles after getting out of Cushing, where they ditched the Thunderbird by driving it into the Cimarron River. Then they stole a Ford F-150 pickup from a retired farmer who lived two miles south of Perkins.

Johnson removed the pickup's tag and stole another tag from a parked vehicle on the river as the owner fished the Cimarron. Now believing they had bought some time, the two decided to go back to Glencoe and get rid of the kid.

Entering town, Johnson and Anderson stopped at the Ross gas station to fill up. Anderson went inside and began a conversation with Leland while fumbling to get an ice-cold Orange Crush from the soda machine. Anderson told Leland that he and Johnson were passing through on their way to Ponca City and had decided to take the back roads to enjoy the scenery. They started discussing Panther basketball, with Leland stressing that the Panthers were undefeated so far in the season.

"So," said Anderson, "they're good. Are there any standouts?"

"They all are," said Leland. "The starters are good, maybe good enough for a couple of them to get a scholarship at a mid-level school. The bench is ready to pick up the slack when called to duty."

"In a town like this what do the kids do for entertainment?" asked Anderson.

"Well, they go to movies or go to the lake, or sometimes they just hang around town on Main. You know, these are the things the kids do," said Leland.

Anderson then commented, "I guess not much happens in a town like this, seems pretty quiet."

"We had a bank robbery a few weeks back," said Leland. "That sure shook things up around here. Lucky for us, Porter saw a strange car on the night of the robbery parked in front of the bank. He told the FBI agents everything he saw," said Leland.

"Where does this Porter kid live? His folks must be pretty proud of him."

"He lives not far from town, but he has been seen jogging quite a bit lately, getting ready for the game against Kaw City," said Leland. Just at that time Porter jogged by the station where Leland saw him and shouted out a hello from the screen door. "So that's him," said Anderson. "He is Porter?" "Yep" said Leland. "He is the one alright."

At that time Johnson stuck his head through the front door of the station and said, "We're ready." Anderson paid the seven dollars and twenty-five cents and then the two of them climbed into the front of the truck and drove away. Anderson then told Johnson that he had seen Porter and knows what he looks like.

Porter had started his regimen of running six miles daily, with the exception of Saturdays. Instead of running the pavement, he was running the country roads. These roads were softer; the dirt gave more, and so he believed dirt roads would strengthen his hamstrings ankles and better condition his overall body. His routine required him to start running each day at 6:00 p.m., keep a pace of ten-minute miles, and be back by 7:00 p.m. easily. After a few days of conditioning, his leg strength and breathing ability were progressing to his liking.

Meanwhile, Anderson and Johnson rented a motel room at the Wagon Wheel Motel on the west edge of Pawnee. The motel was old, having been built in 1914. The exterior and interior walls were made of cinder block that had been painted white. The trim of the Wagon Wheel was done in a maroon. There was a pay telephone in the courtyard, as none of the rooms were equipped with a telephone. Circling the courtyard were wooden-spoke wagon wheels, the kind that were used in the late 1800s on covered wagons. The motel was small, having just eight units, and none of the others were occupied. When the two men rented the room, they paid in cash for a week's stay. Across the street from the Wagon Wheel was a quick-trip store that offered candy bars, chips, sodas, and hot dogs rotating in a steam chamber oven.

Two days after renting the room Anderson and Johnson returned to Glencoe to locate Porter and monitor his routine. They pulled up on Main Street, parked, and then walked into Shell's soda fountain, where they sat down at the counter and ordered hamburgers and ice cream floats.

Just as the burgers were placed in front of the two men the local cop, Alan Downs walked in and took a stool next to Anderson. "I haven't seen you fellas in town before," he said and then extended his hand for a handshake.

For the next ten minutes Anderson and Johnson wondered how much the cop knew about the robbery; they were certain the FBI had plenty of information but were unsure how much the FBI had shared with the local cop. Anderson started a conversation with the officer. "I hear you had a bank robbery not long ago."

"Sure did," said the officer. "Nothing has ever happened here that big since the 1914 fire—or was it in '15? One of those years, anyway, before my time."

"Any suspects?" asked Anderson.

"Not that I know of. I turned the case over to the big boys, you know, the FBI. They get paid big bucks to solve these things," said the cop.

"They sure do; let them work for a change. I mean, we pay their salaries with our tax dollars. In a way you are their boss," said Anderson, by now confident that this cop knew little about the details of the crime, or at least didn't suspect the two strangers he was chatting with.

"You got that right," said the cop.

"I heard a kid may have seen something. Any truth in that?" asked Anderson.

"Yeah, his name is Porter. A good kid. He was hanging around town that night and he got a good look at the car, a blue '66 Thunderbird. Says he saw two of them, both white guys, about five-ten, around your height. One of them was at the bank door, just standing there like it was nobody's business wearing a brim hat like he was a big shot or something. Just standing there waiting on the bank to open."

Anderson then asked, "Does the kid go to high school here in town?"

"Sure does, just down the street. In fact he usually comes in here after school, him and some of his buddies, about 3:15 p.m. every school day."

Anderson looked at his watch; it was 3:10 p.m. "Come on," he said to Johnson. "We need to go." Anderson then shook hands with the cop and said, "It was nice to meet you."

When the two stepped outside, they headed directly to their stolen truck and climbed in. Anderson said, "We'll stay parked here until Porter arrives. We need to see what he looks like up close."

Shortly Anderson and Johnson saw a '63 Galaxy drive up and park across the street. The driver got out and headed toward the fountain. As he was about to go through the door, another car rolled in, and the driver yelled, "Hey, Porter, get us a booth!"

Anderson and Johnson now knew which one was Porter for sure and had gotten a good look at his face. After sitting a few more minutes they pulled away from the curb. "The cop doesn't know anything, but if he comes out and sees us still sitting here, he might think it is strange," said Anderson. "Let's go drive around for a while and then check back later to see if the kid is still here."

They drove away, turned right at the end of Main, and went to the car wash. Johnson got out to wash the truck and soon began cursing when not getting enough soap to clean the truck. Anderson remained in the truck, chain smoking with the windows closed. After fifteen minutes they drove back down Main, where they saw the Galaxy backing up. They stopped to let it get all the way out and then followed it to the intersection of Main and 108. Porter put on his signal light to turn left. The pickup followed at a distance, but close enough to keep the Galaxy in sight.

Once on 108 and out of the city limits, Porter increased his speed to seventy-five, and so did Anderson, but he continued to keep some distance to avoid suspicion. Once Porter reached the Linsenmeyer Corner he turned right onto a dirt road. "He won't lose us," said Anderson. "We can just follow the dust."

When Porter reached his driveway, he pulled up to the garage and parked without entering it. The pickup passed by as Porter was entering the house. Porter saw the truck but did not make a connection between it and men driving it.

"There he is," said Johnson, "What do we do now?"

"Keep going," said Anderson. "We now know where he lives. Keep driving and we will come back in a little while to see if we can find him alone."

At 5:50 p.m. the pickup came back down the road. No one was in the yard, and the car was still parked where Porter had pulled up. Anderson and Johnson knew they could not keep going up and down the dirt road without taking a chance they would be spotted and raising concerns, so they pulled into the driveway. "If we see the kid we will ask for directions to a good fishing hole. He should go for that," said Anderson as he killed the truck's motor.

As he took one step outside the truck, the door to the house opened, and out stepped Porter. "Hi, can I help you?" he asked.

Johnson and Anderson could not help but notice he was wearing a blue and gold sweatshirt, blue sweatpants, and tennis shoes. "Yes," said Anderson, "we are looking for a fishing hole, one that has the granddaddy of all fish, know what I mean?"

Porter smiled and then said, "You are looking for the same hole as me, but I have yet to find the big one. There are some pretty good spots around here, though. Are you guys new to the area?"

"Yes we are, just bought a place in Pawnee. And well, it is a good day to fish, so we are trying to find a spot where we can do a little."

"Try going three-quarters of a mile east of here and then hook a right and go one mile. There you will cross the bridge; just under it is the best place I have found," said Porter. "Me and my friends go there to fish and swim; it's a good place to do both."

"Thanks," said Anderson. "You have been very helpful."

Johnson and Anderson returned to the truck and began backing out of the driveway. Once on the dirt road they headed east as the kid had told them. They stopped at the next intersection, a mile down the road, to discuss what to do next.

CHAPTER 18

Tragedy and Opportunity

Sunday morning most of the townspeople dressed in their Sunday finest dress clothes to attend one of the four churches in town. Porter met Mike, Becky, Randy, and Larry in the parking lot and then entered the building, where they found a pew in the back of the church. As the congregation settled in Kenneth Shell rose from the first pew and went to the podium, where he stood while taking a handkerchief from his back pocket. The crowd became fidgety as they waited for Reverend Stockton to come in from the side door. He would always enter the sanctuary and take a seat behind the podium until the last hymn was sung. He would then go to the podium, where he would deliver the Sunday message.

Today, Kenneth Shell got up and stood overlooking the reverend's flock. He slowly began to speak. "Last night I received a call from a detective with the Dallas Police Department. He told me the reverend, his wife, and their two children had been murdered while on vacation. The detective believes it was a robbery gone badly; they died quickly but not without a fight." Shell went on, "The detective found my name, address, and telephone number in Reverend Stockton's wallet in case of an emergency."

The congregation listened to Shell's words in disbelief. The crowd gasped for air the more they were told. Shell then said in tribute to the Stockton family there would be no sermon on this Sunday, "But rather, let us sing songs from the hymnal book and say prayers for the souls of these fine Christian people." Then Shell asked they each take the hymnal in front of them and turn to page 222, where they found and began to sing "Amazing Grace."

When church ended the worshipers were slow to leave the parking lot. Groups formed to talk about the Stockton family; many spoke about the kindness of the family as well as their generosity. Others said when the police found the scum responsible they intended to attend the trial to make sure justice was carried out. The loss of the fine family was one more infliction of tragedy to the Glencoe community.

Porter left church and returned home, ate lunch with his family, and then returned to Main Street, where he met up with some of the guys. The fountain was open so they settled in to play some pool, listen to the jukebox, and have a good time.

After a few minutes Anderson and Johnson walked in; they knew where Porter was because they had trailed him. They sat down at the fountain bar, and after ordering a cold cut sandwich, Anderson got up and went to the back of the fountain, where Porter and his friends were. As soon as Porter saw Anderson he said, "Good to see you again. Have any luck catching the big one?"

Anderson went over to Porter and ignored the question, instead saying, "The lady behind the cash register where we got gas said you are a hero."

"Oh, you must be talking about the bank robbery. Nope, not a hero just told the cops what I saw, that's all."

"Well everyone in these parts sure considers you to be a brave guy. I mean, you got a good look at the hombres, didn't you?"

"Well it's hard to say, but I think if they put some people in a lineup I could pick one of them out, the one who was standing next to the bank door."

"That's good, kid," said Anderson, and then he walked back to the bar, took a stool, and sat back down. "I just talked with the kid; says he thinks he can pick me out from a lineup," he told Johnson, and then he began to laugh.

At 4:00 p.m. Porter left the fountain. He and Mike went for a drive around town, and then they decided to make a run to Perkins to check out pretty girls. As they entered town Porter wanted to run by Phil Hughes's house; he and Phil had been friends ever since the Glencoe Baptist Church and Perkins Baptist Church had shared a cabin at Falls Creek, a Southern Baptist church camp, two years earlier. On the first night Phil and Porter had hit it off, and soon they had become good friends. After the evening services they would hook up with a date they had prearranged sometime during the day. The boys and girls were not permitted to swim together, but that did not keep the two young men from spying on the girls on occasion. When they knew the chaperone was gone for a short while they made a panty run on one of the girls' cabins. On another occasion both boys had set up seven dates each, all to occur on the same night.

Arriving at the Hughes residence, the two got out of the car, went to the big front porch of the white house, and rang the doorbell. Suzy, sister to Phil and one year younger, answered the door. Porter asked if Phil was around, and she went and got him. The three met on the front porch to discuss what they could do in town while they were there. Phil suggested they drag Main to see if any girls were out cruising.

As they drove down Main Phil began to honk at a '64 Falcon being driven by a cute brunette with two other girls in the car with her. As soon as they saw Phil they motioned for him to pull over. Phil waved in a fashion that said, follow me. They then drove around the block and parked in the school parking lot. As the girls drove up Phil told Porter and Mike the girls were hot and always looking for somebody from out of town to hang with. "Stay cool said Phil.

When the girls exited the car, Phil took two of them with one of his arms and the other with the other and escorted them to where his friends stood. "Gentlemen, I would like to introduce you to some of Perkins's finest women. This is Lael Russell, Jan Stigler, and Beth Oaks."

Porter introduced himself and Mike and asked the girls if they would like to ride around for a while. The girls agreed, and in the front with Porter was Jan Stigler, while in the back seat were Mike and Phil with Beth and Lael. They continued to drag Main for a while before they decided to try to find some beer. "The only place where we can get any is at the honk and holler," said Phil, "but we will have to get someone to buy it for us." Phil then remembered that Chris Lockwood was in town, home on leave from the Army. "I saw Chris a little while back. Let's find him and see if he will get us what we need."

As they drove the streets they saw Chris and flagged him down and told them their story. Chris agreed to buy the beer, "But you have to say here; don't come near the store or they will know I am buying for you."

Once they had the beer they drove to Wild Horse Canyon, where they popped open a couple and started drinking. The more they drank, the more the girls began to open up, talk about anything and everything. Mike and Lael became friendly and made plans to meet up again on the following Saturday night. Lael was a beautiful brunette and fell head over heels for Mike. As the sun began going down, the girls said they had to get back home, so the boys drove them to their car where Mike let out the other girls and drove Lael home. After Mike returned the three, Phil, Mike and Porter agreed to meet again in a week in Stillwater, where they could continue the hunt for girls and Mike would have his date with Lael. As Porter was driving away, he yelled back at Phil, "Bring that cute sister of yours along next time."

The two entered Glencoe and headed toward Main Street and parked, coincidentally next to Anderson and Johnson in their pickup. Mike looked to Porter and asked, "Are those the same two guys you spoke to earlier?"

"Yeah. They said they have a place in Pawnee, but it seems like they are spending quite a bit of time here."

All four got out of their vehicles at the same time, and Anderson said, "Good to see you."

"Yeah, how are you guys?" asked Porter.

"I am glad we ran into you," said Anderson. "Me and my partner are thinking about setting up a little shop over at the lake—you know, sell bait, snacks, beer, fishing tackle, and in time sell fishing permits and maybe state fishing licenses. But we need somebody to work part time, and frankly, you seem like a good kid, and we wanted to give you first shot at it. Minimum wage is two dollars an hour, but we are willing to pay two dollars and twenty-five cents. You would work on weekends, holidays, and after school—except, of course, when you have a basketball game or practice after school. So what do you say?"

Porter liked the idea of earning extra spending money, and in the summer he could work there, fish, and most importantly, not haul hay. "Maybe," he finally said. "But I need to talk to my folks about it."

"Sure," said Anderson, "give it some thought, and I will get back to you. I would like to open it next week, so in a day or so I will check back."

CHAPTER 19

On the Eve of A Championship

DURING PRACTICE WALLACE HAD the substitutes playing the five starters in a man-to-man defense. It wasn't long before Porter caught a sharp elbow to his jaw while going for a rebound, resulting in the loosening of two teeth. He left practice early to go to his dentist in Stillwater, who looked at the problem and told him he needed to see a specialist in Oklahoma City, Dr. Marsha Tartar. Dr. Tartar was accustomed to receiving referrals from other doctors, and she scheduled the appointment for the following day. Tartar was known to have skill and precision and had seen many basketball and football players during the course of her medical career.

After arriving at the dentist's office, Porter was met by the receptionist, Angela. She told him they were expecting him and then escorted him to a dental chair located off the hall leading to the doctor's office. Dr. Tartar was summoned, and she came out to meet Porter. "Well hello," she said. "I hear you may have a couple of teeth giving you a problem. We will start with X-rays and then go from there. Can I get you something to read?"

"No," said Porter, "I am fine."

One of the technicians came into the room and introduced herself as Misty. She said, "Hi there. I am going to take the X-rays, so put this in your mouth and hold your breath until I say to exhale." After taking the picture, Misty came back into the room to look inside Porter's mouth. 'Hmm, I think you will be just fine," she concluded, smiling.

After the numbing took effect Dr. Tartar came back in and said, "I have looked at the X-rays, and I believe they confirm my early assessment that this is not a major problem, and we can get it fixed with a little time." After further probing Porter's mouth, the doctor asked Misty to prepare an upper and lower mouth brace. "Porter, I want you to wear these mouth guards for two weeks, day and night. They will give your teeth time to heal and re-set. Do you think you can do that?" she asked.

"Before you leave today I want you to meet with our dental hygienist, Janna. She can advise you how to care for your teeth, strengthen them and make them stronger in the event you are elbowed again or sustain an injury to the mouth, will you do that?" asked Tartar. "Sure," said Porter. At about that same time Janna came into the room and introduced herself. "Dr. Tartar said you are a basketball player, is that right?" asked the technician. "Well, I try," said Porter. "Okay, then let's make sure your mouth guard fits appropriately and then you can leave."

Porter agreed he wouldn't have any problem with the solutions offered by Dr. Tartar and her staff and then proceeded to leave the dentist office.

The next day in practice the team continued preparations for the championship game. Since before the Kaw City game Coach Wallace had kept his players running and honing their free throw skills. Wallace had reviewed the film on each game Morrison had played, and he knew Morrison had the complete package: they could shoot long range and pound the ball in the paint. Wallace had to make a decision on how best to defend Morrison—let them have the low-percentage long shot, which had the potential to beat his team if they were hot, or guard against the inside the paint shots under the basket. He pondered the question and came to the conclusion to allow the long-distance shot be the one to beat his Panthers.

One week away from the showdown, the team practices were not going as well as Coach Wallace wanted. His players were missing too many shots, both at the free throw line and from the top of the key. Additionally, the substitutes were outplaying the starters on defense. Wallace was concerned early in the week and grew more tense by midweek, seeing little improvement.

On Thursday night, with one day left before the biggest game of the year, the townspeople and Wallace met at the Senior Citizens Center for the final time during the basketball season. Wallace thanked everyone for the support he and his players had received every since the beginning of the season. He assured the crowd his players would be ready to take home the championship trophy while not mentioning how badly practices had gone during the week. Wallace then gave an injury report, including telling those present about Porter's jaw, but he assured them he was ready to play and had not been slowed on the court since his injury.

When asked how he intended to defend against the powerful Northern Division champs Wallace would only say, "It will be a challenge to our players and to my own coaching skills. Come watch the game and you can see for yourself." Wallace told the fans he depended on their enthusiasm and energy each game to keep both himself and his players "ramped up." The coach ended by saying that Morrison's dominance of the conference was about to come to an end, and the Panthers' losing streak of twenty years was also coming to an end. The crowd exploded with thunderous applause and cheers.

While Wallace and the townspeople were meeting, the players were gathered at Bill's home to discuss among them what had been plaguing them during practice. Shell mentioned they could not compete effectively if they continued to play like they had been in practice. Bill said he thought it was just nerves, and when one of them was not playing well, the rest were not picking up the slack. Lyle said that in past games one player could be down, but the slack was picked up by others, and the team needed to be more focused. The players' meeting lasted for two hours.

Afterward, Porter, Mike Crawford, Jimmy Arias, and Mike Phillips met on Main Street to talk more about the attitude of the team, how they could settle their nerves, and how each could take individual responsibility to be more proactive. As they continued to talk, the group saw Anderson and Johnson approaching in their pickup. At the time the only people on Main Street were the four of them.

"Hey, Porter, isn't that your friends?" asked Mike Phillips.

"Well I don't know that I would call them friends, but I do know them," said Porter.

The pickup slowed down and then parked. Anderson and Johnson got out, approached the four, and asked Porter if he had decided to work for them at the bait and tackle shop at Lone Chimney Lake. Porter told them he would but could not start until Saturday. "You know, we have the conference championship tomorrow, Friday night," he added. "But what time do you want me to start work on Saturday?"

"How about 2:00 p.m.?" said Anderson "Just meet us and we will run you over there, get you set up, and then you can take it from there. Meet us at Walt's Corner."

"Okay," said Porter. "See you on Saturday."

As Anderson and Johnson drove away, they commented to one another about how easy it was going to be to grab Porter and dispose of him. "No one is going to miss him," said Johnson. "Everyone knows he will be working, and when we get rid of him, it will be hours before anyone knows he has gone missing." The two laughed and kept on driving.

The FBI headquarters in Oklahoma City had issued pictures of Anderson and Johnson to the newspapers and television stations in a five-state radius. They wanted the public to know about the criminals. All around the region newscasters reported, "These two men, Gerald Anderson and Leroy Johnson, should be considered to be armed and dangerous. They will not hesitate to use violence."

CHAPTER 20

Renewed Hope

FRIDAY NIGHT THE PANTHER boys met at the school gym two hours before their scheduled departure time. For the first hour the players and Coach Wallace went over the game plan for the final time, and then Wallace asked each player to state what the championship game meant to them individually. He wanted them to speak about what teamwork meant and why each player had decided to play basketball at an early age. Wallace was clearly trying to motivate his team and get them emotionally ready to play.

After the players had finished, he gave a detailed account of each game they had played up to the championship game. He told them how the odds had been stacked against them since the beginning of the year and how they had fought together to beat teams that were better than they were, at least on paper. "You made it this far because you have played as a team, played with confidence, and because you believe in each other. You have a gift, skill, ability, and most of all; you have a determination that comes from your hearts. Play with these gifts and you will walk away tonight, regardless of the outcome, with pride."

Wallace ended by telling the players to go to the locker room to pack their suits and equipment. After packing, the players loaded the bus with their duffle bags and then came back into the gym. As they sat on the bench where they sat every home game, the townspeople began to come into the gymnasium. The various crowd members were carrying signs, shouting words of encouragement, and holding one finger in the air, indicating they believed the Panthers were number one in the state.

After they settled in the bleachers, Coach Wallace told the fans, "Before we leave, I want to give you an opportunity to say a few words." He then pointed to the stage, where a microphone had been set up.

Bill Childers, Frank Driskel, and Kenneth Shell walked to the stage, where they stood. First up was Bill; he went to the microphone and told the players, the coach, and the fans that the team had made believers of every one of them. "You have made this town proud," he said, and then he turned the microphone over to Frank.

Frank told everyone within earshot how the team had brought renewed hope to the town and its people. "We are proud of each and every one of you," he proclaimed.

Last up was Kenneth, who told the players that the people stood with them and would support them at the game a hundred percent, from when they first stepped on the court until the final buzzer went off.

Following the comments, Wallace gave his parting words to the crowd: "Thanks to everyone who has supported us, and just know that however this thing turns out tonight, we will leave it all on the floor and leave with our heads held high." The players, led by Coach Wallace, then departed the gym, walked down the hall, and exited the school, where they boarded the bus.

The players took one bus, while on another were the cheerleaders, pom-pom girls, and the Lady Panthers, who had lost their title chance after being beaten by the Ralston Tigers. The girls had played full-out, but when Lynne Sawyer had sprained her ankle in the second half and Linda Childers had fouled out of the game, the team was not able to bounce back. Even so, they fought until the buzzer ended the game with the Lady Panthers trailing by two points. The girls and Wallace were pleased at how the team had played better than anyone had expected throughout the year and even more pleased that all the starters would return in 1968 as pre-season conference favorites.

CHAPTER 21

Leave It All on the Court

Upon arriving in Perkins, a neutral site for the championship game the players were feeling good about the support they'd received from the Glencoe townspeople; they were anticipating a tough game, and it never escaped their minds that they had not beaten Morrison in years. As they entered the gym, the crowds for both teams were equal in number and enthusiasm. Coach Wallace met with the players in the locker room, gave them some food for thought, and then told them to go on the court and begin their warm-up.

Throughout the first half both schools played all-out defense. The Panthers would switch from man-to-man and go into a zone in an effort to keep Morrison off balance. Morrison, on the other hand, played a man-to-man defense while also applying full-court pressure. Bill, who considered Morrison an archenemy because of his lackluster performance in the game with them the year before, had a grudge to settle.

He wanted to not only become conference champions but also wanted to be selected to the conference all-star team as one of the five starters. He still believed the Morrison game had prevented his dream from coming true last year, when he was selected as a second-team member.

Bill had the height advantage in the paint but was having difficulty getting the ball because of Morrison's man-to-man defense. Every time the Panthers would look for Bill under the goal and pass to him, the opposing players collapsed on him, forcing the ball to go back outside. Seeing this in the middle of the first half, Wallace called time-out. "We have been trying to work the ball in to Bill," he said. "Let's keep that up, but Bill; I want you to kick the ball to the corner as they come inside whenever you touch it. Our corners have been free to take the shot."

As Glencoe brought the ball down court they went with that plan. Shell, who normally plays as a small forward, took the first pass out from Bill in the paint, set his feet, and let it fly; he scored, tying the game. On defense the Panthers continued with the game plan of letting Morrison have the outside shot and preventing shots in the paint. Their defensive play continued to be strong and continued to confuse Morrison, with their quick changes. At halftime the two teams were tied at 42 points apiece.

In the locker room Wallace had high praise for his players. "You are playing smart and shooting 50 percent from the field, but it has to get better. They now know we will kick the ball out every time Bill touches it, so let's change things up. Bill, I want you to take shots in the paint; maybe we can get their big man in foul trouble and score from the line."

When the second half began, Bill did take more shots under the goal, and each time with success. Now Morrison was even more confused, thinking, do we cover Bill and allow the long shot or continue to cover our man in the man-to-man defense? The Morrison coach took a time-out and told his players to stop Bill and let the Panthers have the long shot. Bill was being too successful getting and hitting high-percentage shots on the inside.

The Panthers and the Morrison Tigers kept up a fast-paced game, the two schools acted as though they were in a heavyweight fight, standing toe-to-toe at times while always on the move at other times. As the second half was nearing its end, the two teams remained deadlocked at 65 points each. Morrison inbounded the ball and went for a long two; they scored, taking the lead. The Panthers went down court, continuing to face the full-court press. Shell saw Lyle open as he cut through the paint, the first time a Panther player had entered the paint except for Bill, to try to retrieve a rebound. Lyle's defender was screened out by Bill, Shell made the pass, and Lyle had an easy left-handed layup. Again the game was tied, now with thirty seconds left on the clock.

Wallace quickly called time-out and met the players at the bench. "Play smart," he told them. "No fouls, and if they miss their shot get the rebound. Shell, on a defensive rebound race to our end, and the rest of you look for him."

Both teams were now out of time-outs. As Morrison brought the ball downcourt with thirty seconds, left they began to pass from one player to another, playing patiently and looking for a good shot. With seven seconds left a player launched a shot at the top of the key. As the player let the ball fly, he was fouled by a Panther player. "Two shots," announced the referee.

The Morrison player went to the free throw line, feeling the pressure to make both shots so the Panthers could at best tie, not win, with a last-second attempt. He took the first and hit all net. He took the ball for his second try, gazed at the rim, and slowly raised his arms while holding the ball. His shot bounced off the rim and into the hands of Lyle.

While going for the rebound, Lyle saw Porter streaking downcourt—three seconds left. He turned and threw the ball as hard as he could to Porter who caught it in the air, took one step, and made the layup as the buzzer sounded, ending the game. The Panthers had won by one point.

The crowds for both teams cheered as they recognized both schools had played hard. The Glencoe fans were going wild, slapping each other on the backs and congratulating one another as if they had played the game themselves. As the Panther players celebrated with their coach, the fans came onto the court. After a few minutes the scorekeeper announced via microphone for everyone to leave the court; it was time to award the conference championship trophy.

As the fans went back to the bleachers, the players for both teams went to their respective benches, where they sat down. The announcer then introduced Morrison as the conference runner-ups and gave them a silver trophy. The Glencoe fans cheered the Tigers as they received the trophy.

"Next we have a trophy for the champions. Will the Panthers come to the center of the court?" said the scorekeeper.

The players went to center court, Wallace joining them and accepting the trophy. He said, "I will accept this trophy on behalf of the players, the townspeople, who gave us so much support, and the parents of these kids, who stood with them during the difficult practices and while on our journey here tonight. The game was hard-fought, and tonight everyone here saw two great teams play their hearts out. There are no losers tonight."

CHAPTER 22

Are You Ready to Die?

SATURDAY MORNING PORTER GOT out of bed feeling sore and bruised. The game had taken a physical toll on both teams' players. Porter was proud of the accomplishments his team had made during the basketball season and was ready for baseball season to begin in thirty days, a sport he could excel in.

But today he didn't have the same amount of time as he did most Saturdays, as he was scheduled to work at the bait and tackle shop. After taking a shower and getting dressed, he made a few phone calls to his buddies and planned on meeting around eight that evening in town, where they would gather and then head to Stillwater to celebrate their conference championship. Porter did not know how long he would be working, but because it was still winter he figured it wouldn't be more than three or four hours, which would give him plenty of time to clean up and join the gang for what would become the best party of the year.

At the scheduled hour Porter met Anderson and Johnson at Walt's Corner. "Hey, kid, come get in with us and we will take you over to the shop," said Anderson.

Porter climbed into the truck, and the three headed toward the lake. After they had driven for fifteen minutes Anderson steered the truck into the pasture containing the swimming and fishing hole Porter had first told them about. "Why are we going this way?" he asked. "This isn't near the lake; you need to turn around and go east."

"We know," said Johnson, "but there is something we have to do first." Coming to a complete stop, the two got out, followed by Porter. "Over here," said Johnson. "This is what we want to show you."

Just as Johnson spoke, Anderson went behind Porter and put his right arm around the young man's neck. Porter tried to fight back, but the harder he fought, the more pressure Anderson applied. Johnson took Porter's wrists and tied them together with string used to bind bales of hay, then Anderson forced him to a small campsite the two had prearranged. He threw Porter to the ground and said that unless he cooperated he would be killed. At that moment Johnson pulled a pistol, and Porter heard the gun cock.

Porter lying on the cold, hard ground, asked, "Who are you? Why am I here? Why have you tied me up?"

"You don't know who you are dealing with, do you? And you think you could identify me if I was in a lineup—does that help any?" asked Anderson.

"You robbed the bank," said Porter.

"Smart kid," Johnson added.

"So now let's do what we came here for," said Anderson. "Kid, if you want to live, you will answer the questions I am going to ask. Otherwise your time runs out."

The criminal paused and sighed before finally asking, "What did you tell the FBI?"

"Only that I saw a strange car in town," replied Porter.

"Look, kid, don't play games. You told them more; now what did you say?"

"Okay, okay. I said I saw a Thunderbird, a 1966 model, blue with a white top."

"And how did you describe me?" Anderson asked.

"I said there was a guy at the door, five-foot-ten or so, wearing a hat with a brim."

Anderson nodded. "Okay, that's it. Johnson, do what we came for."

Johnson moved behind Porter and put the gun to his head, cocked the hammer, and pulled the trigger. *Click* went the gun. Porter, sweating, knew the gun had not fired. He thought to himself thankfully, *I am alive*!

Johnson again cocked the hammer, frustrated, but a truck came driving slowly down the road and turned into the pasture. Anderson saw it and told Johnson to put the gun away. Porter was quickly untied and told not to say a word. Pulling up to where Anderson had parked his pickup, the driver got out and asked what they were doing on his property.

"We came here to fish," said Anderson. "We heard this is a good hole, got the big one in it."

The farmer looked at Anderson and said, "See that no trespassing sign by the gate? It means what it says; you are trespassing, so get off my land." Anderson then apologized, and the three of them climbed back in the truck and drove off.

As they drove away, the farmer took off his John Deere cap and scratched his head, recalling seeing a certain picture in the local paper. It was a man who looked like the one he'd just spoken to. He hurriedly got back in his vehicle and drove home, where he called the FBI.

Anderson and Johnson knew they'd had a close call and decided in was in their best interest to get rid of the kid quickly. But they had to find a new location. As they continued driving, they came to the intersection of Highway 108 and 52000 East Road. They crossed over the highway and drove west, coming to a one-lane country bridge. The location was isolated and, by the look of it the country road was not heavily traveled. Porter recognized the bridge and the road, as this was the way he would run each day during basketball season to get in shape.

"FBI office," answered the receptionist when the farmer called. "May I help you?"

The farmer began to tell his story about what he had just encountered, but the receptionist stopped him and said she was going to transfer his call to lead FBI Agent Ferguson in charge of solving the crime. The agent took the information, including a full description of the two men as well as Porter. He also took down the exact location where the farmer had seen them as well as the information about the vehicle they were driving. After hanging up, the agent called his partner, who was in Stillwater following up with Ms. Anderson, and told him of the news. "Get a couple more agents and check it out immediately," said the lead agent.

The agent in Stillwater, Steve Turner then got into his unmarked, black LTD and drove to Glencoe, where he had agreed to meet the farmer at the café. The agent and farmer sat down at a table, ordered coffee, and began to discuss what the farmer knew. At that moment Mike Phillips walked in. He recognized the agent and could tell from the expression on both men's faces that the conversation was serious. Mike overheard much of the conversation and knew danger was in the air.

The agent left after two additional agents arrived on the scene. Mike remained in the café and went over to the farmer. "Are you okay? You seem a little upset," said Mike.

"I am, I just saw the bank robbers, and they had a kid with them; I think they are going to kill him. Said they were going fishing, but I don't think that was why they were there. I never saw any fishing poles."

Mike then asked where he had seen the criminals, and the farmer told him, at the fishing hole. Mike quickly figured out it was Porter they had. He left the café in a hurry and went to the fountain, where he called Bill Hodge, Mike Crawford, Jimmy Arias, and a few others. As he hung up after the last call, his girlfriend, Melodie Alleman, walked in. "Hi, sweetie. What's wrong?"

Mike told Melodie what he had learned and that he was getting together some people to go look for Porter. Melodie asked if she could join the hunt. "I don't know," said Mike. "This could get dangerous."

At that time Warden came driving up in his Mustang, and Mike told him what happened. Warden got Mike and Melodie into his car and drove to pick up Bill, who had already put the word out to Randy and Becky, who also joined the hunt. As they drove toward the fishing hole, they were met by Mary Ann. "Where could they have taken him?" asked Arias.

"Let's backtrack," Mike. "They will be around here somewhere, along the back roads, so let's go."

They split up and searched the back roads, going different directions. Suddenly Warden saw what he believed to be a pickup hidden in a clump of trees. He told the others he was going to park a quarter mile back, and they could sneak up on whoever was there.

As they slowly made their way to the bridge, they began to hear noises coming from under the bridge. "Quiet, they are under there," Warden said as he pointed to the location of the noise. "Phillips, you go around to the other side, and I will come in from this side."

As they crept closer. Warden saw Porter and saw he was tied up. Anderson was just about to take out his pistol when Phillips slipped, making enough noise for the bank robbers to hear and see him. As the two ran toward Phillips, Warden came flying in and grabbed Anderson. The two struggled while Phillips was taking on Johnson. Melodie, who had stayed back from the bridge, heard the noise and ran toward the commotion. She saw what was happening and went to Porter and untied him. Now free, Porter rushed toward Anderson, jumping on him to help Warden subdue the man.

Just at that time the other cars that had been searching came along and saw Melodie standing in the road, screaming. Everyone got out of their cars and ran to the scene. Lynne Sawyer, who was with Randy, grabbed a rock and hit Johnson in the head. Phillips was able to gain control of the struggle and hit Johnson with a hard right to the jaw, knocking the thief to the ground. He yelled to Randy to get a rope; Randy always carried rope in his car, which he used at the swimming hole to tie to a tree limb so the kids could swing out and land in the cool, deep water for fun.

Randy came back, and he and Phillips tied up Johnson. Porter and Warden had knocked out Anderson. They tied him up next and dragged him back to Randy's car, where they loaded him into the backseat. Porter had taken possession of the gun, and he rode with Randy to make sure the two did not get away.

After getting the two into the car, Warden walked over to Porter and, to everyone's surprise, hit him with a left hook square on the jaw. Warden looked at Porter on the ground, said, "Now it's over," and smiled.

They returned to Glencoe and went straight to the police station, where they woke up the cop, who had fallen asleep at his desk. Arias told the deputy they had caught the bank robbers and had them bound. "Where are they?" asked the cop.

"In the car; maybe you should call someone so they can be locked up."

The cop stepped outside, saw the robbers, and gaped in disbelief; he recognized the two as the same men he sat with in the fountain a few days earlier. He said, "I thought you two looked suspicious. I was keeping an eye on you; you can't fool a good investigator like myself. It was only a matter of time until I could prove you did the robbery, and then I was going to take you in myself."

The cop then called the Payne County sheriff's office, which dispatched a deputy to take the two men into custody and transfer them to the county jail.

That afternoon before sundown, the FBI agents returned to Glencoe and met with all who had been involved in the capture of the two fugitives. "You are brave young men and women," said the agent, "but very foolish. You could have been killed." The agent then questioned each of them and questioned Porter in detail. The FBI had gotten what they wanted, an arrest. Time had run out for the crooks.

CHAPTER 23

Good-bye

As the school year ended, Mike Crawford, Orville, and Wesley kept their pact with Uncle Sam and entered military service. The three of them were sent to boot camp together as they had been promised. For three months Porter never heard from them, but he was told by Mike's brother, Ronnie, they had completed boot camp and been sent to Fort Bragg, North Carolina, where they were receiving technical and survival training.

The town had experienced a lot in the months prior to there enlistment. They'd had a bank robbery and had won the Santa Fe Basketball Conference. They lost in the regional to Olive but had given the townspeople plenty to be excited about.

Mary Ann continued to date the guy she had met in Stillwater, Jon, while Keith and Rhonda maintained a steady relationship of their own. Kay and Luke finally hooked up, as did Linda Treat and Charles Robinson. Linda Childers continued to have boys over every weeknight to watch Bonanza, always a different boy each week. Becky Clark broke up with her boyfriend but did not seem upset, as each weekend night she was popular with the out-of-town boys. Randy met a girl from Pawnee, and the two hung out together every chance they got. Rhonda and Max married a few years later; Leland and Brenda continued to run a successful business; Warden and Marietta never dated again, but that was okay with both of them. Mike Phillips moved to Lake Keystone near Tulsa, while Melodie moved to Bartlesville to start a business and raise a family. Jimmy Arias went to OSU on a wrestling scholarship. And Porter, he continued his life as if nothing had ever happened. Overall, life continued as it always had.

Two months after Mike, Wesley, and Orville had left for Fort Bragg, Porter received a call one night around ten. "Hey, bro, it's Mike! Here with me are Wes and Orville; we just got our orders, its Vietnam."

Porter listened to his friend while a tear formed in his eye. He knew all along that was where they would end up, fighting for their very own survival. He did not know whether any of the three would return but did know that if anyone could make it, they would. As they hung up all Porter could say to his friend was, "Good-bye, I will see you guys when you get back."

2011 Doctors Building Glencoe Oklahoma 300

Entrance to Yost Lake 300

Glencoe senior Citizens center in 2011 300

Pawnee National Guard Armory 300

About the Author

In 1967 I was a teenager in Glencoe, Oklahoma, population four hundred twenty. That same year there was a bank robbery in which I was able to provide to FBI agents a description of one suspicious person, who became a prime suspect in the robbery. While this was a major event for the small town, life continued to go forward, with sports being the main topic of conversation. Around that same year, the high school was vandalized, and all the high school students became suspects. As an athlete I enjoyed the opportunity to participate in both baseball and basketball and enjoy the fruits of victory while learning valuable lessons through losses.

After high school I attended Oklahoma State University and majored in Sociology. Upon graduation I became involved in state government, primarily working with juvenile delinquents, children of abuse and neglect, and persons afflicted with mental illness. I have lived in Oklahoma City since 1993 and am married to Linda Stecker Smith. I have two biological children, Kimberly Porter-Russell and

Keri Lynn Porter-Warmuth, and two stepchildren, Adam Smith and Allison Smith.

Life has been *good*!